MATTHEW REILLY

COBALT BLUE

MATTHEW REILLY

COBALT BLUE

ORION

First published in Great Britain in 2023 by Orion Fiction,
an imprint of The Orion Publishing Group Ltd.,
Carmelite House, 50 Victoria Embankment
London EC4Y 0DZ

An Hachette UK Company

1 3 5 7 9 10 8 6 4 2

Illustrations on pages 7, 169 and 176 by MARTIN MERCER
Map illustrations on pages 28 and 115 by IRONGAV

A CIP catalogue record for this book is
available from the British Library.

ISBN (Hardback) 978 1 3987 1606 3
ISBN (Export Trade Paperback) 978 1 3987 1843 2
ISBN (eBook) 978 1 3987 1608 7

Printed and bound in Great Britain by Clays Ltd, Elcograf S.p.A.

MIX
Paper from
responsible sources
FSC® C104740
FSC
www.fsc.org

www.orionbooks.co.uk

For Kate and Dido

There once was a man selling spears and shields.

About his spears he said, 'They are so
sharp they can pierce anything!'

About his shields he boasted, 'My shields
are so solid, nothing can dent them.'

Then a customer asked him, 'What if I were
to throw your spear at your shield?'

The seller could not respond.

CHINESE PHILOSOPHICAL STORY FROM THE
HAN FEIZI, 3RD CENTURY B.C.

What happens when the irresistible force
meets the immoveable object?

UNKNOWN

SOMEWHERE IN THE ARCTIC CIRCLE
35 YEARS AGO

They found it half buried in the snow about a thousand miles from the North Pole, still steaming from its violent re-entry.

It was a satellite, its curved aluminium sides dented from innumerable debris strikes in the hellish Venusian atmosphere and charred black from the heat of re-entering Earth's.

It lay at the end of a long straight trench that had been created by its high-velocity landing.

The two members of the search team who found it, Dr Cobalt from America and Sergeant Furin from Russia, were peering at it when abruptly a superhot panel on the side of the steaming satellite sprang open and the two of them were enveloped in a sudden cloud of gas.

They both coughed and gagged as they inhaled the

strange gas before dropping to the snowy ground, unconscious.

When they awoke in their respective countries three months later, they would both be very different from their former selves.

They would be very different from every other human being on the planet.

35 YEARS LATER

WASHINGTON, D.C.
0900 HOURS, TODAY

The sonic boom he created over the capital made the whole city shake.

Anyone out on the streets—locals walking in parks, tourists standing outside the various memorials and museums of D.C.—all looked up to see him come rocketing out of the morning sky like a streaking red laser.

It was a sight every American had seen before on television—in Crimea, Ukraine, Hungary—but never, *never*, inside the borders of their own country.

A flying man dressed in red and wearing his signature hood over a grilled ceramic facemask.

He flew like a bullet over the Potomac before pausing to circle high above D.C.

The experts on TV figured he must have come most of the way under the surface of the Atlantic—probably on board a Russian nuclear submarine, during the past few days as America had been mourning the death of Cobalt—because he wasn't picked up by Air Force radars until he was a few miles out of D.C. and it was too late.

It was 9:00 a.m., Monday.

Then he stopped circling, flew sharply downward and, flying at incredible speed, sliced off the top of the Washington Monument.

That was when all the onlookers began screaming and running for their lives.

THE FURY OF RUSSIA

OFFICES OF THE JET PROPULSION LABORATORY, DOWNTOWN LOS ANGELES
0600 HOURS (0900 IN D.C.)

On the west coast, it was still early. Dawn was breaking.

Cassie Cassowitz sat in her deserted office at the Jet Propulsion Laboratory in L.A., tensely watching the live news from Washington, D.C. Her shift, the night shift, was almost over.

Cassie watched the decapitation of the Washington Monument with more horror than the average American citizen. And that was saying something.

On the TV, the commentators were speaking rapidly:

'—*After the sad death of Cobalt last week and the funeral yesterday, it didn't take long for the Russians to strike*—'

'—*He said he would do it and now he has. Cobalt's long-time rival, the Fury of Russia, declared last Tuesday that when Cobalt was in the ground, he would attack*

8

America "immediately and without remorse". He hit Washington, D.C. this morning at 9:00 a.m. local time—'

'—The President has been moved to an undisclosed location after Air Force defences proved useless against the Fury—'

'—the Vice President issued a statement from San Francisco where he was scheduled to attend a private fundraising dinner tonight: "I urge all Americans to pray for our brave heroes. May God give them the strength to save us from this evil man—"'

Cassie stared slack-jawed at the television. The Fury hadn't even waited one whole day.

The great Cobalt's funeral had only been yesterday.

Of course, it had been an enormous affair, a full state funeral with a horse-drawn carriage bearing the mighty hero's coffin down the centre of D.C., flanked by hundreds of military personnel.

Cassie Cassowitz was 29 and an aerospace engineer working in J.P.L.'s satellite division. It was classified government work—spy sats—which made it perfect for her.

It kept her out of sight. It was also literally illegal for anyone to ask her questions. In addition, she worked the night shift, to keep her extra hidden from the world.

Today, like most days, she wore blue jeans and a white zippered pullover with the J.P.L. logo embroidered on the chest.

Just then, one of the TV commentators said something that seized Cassie's attention.

'—*All eyes are now watching to see if D.C.'s resident hero, Cobalt Green, will appear*—'

Her cell phone rang, making her jump. The screen read: TREY.

Cassie answered it. 'Hey.'

'You watching this?' her husband asked.

'Uh-huh.'

'Is Green in D.C.?'

'Yeah.'

'At the White House?' Trey asked.

'Pentagon,' Cassie said. 'Last I heard. You still at home?'

Trey said, 'Yes, I woke up to see all this on the news.'

Then one of the newsreaders on the television exclaimed, '*Wait! Wait! We have a visual on the Fury!*'

And there he was on the TV, standing outside the Pentagon.

Dressed in Kremlin red from head to toe, his ballistic mesh bodysuit and Kevlar armour covering his enormous muscular frame.

The yellow hammer-and-sickle of his country's past empire stood out proudly on his left breast and right shoulderplate.

He was a gigantic specimen of a man, at least six foot

six, hulking, huge, like a professional wrestler. He'd been big before the incident in the Arctic had given him his powers, but he seemed even bigger now.

His head was covered by a dark maroon hood and a savage-looking carbon-ceramic facemask that doubled as an oxygen breather for high-altitude flying.

Right now, his mask's visor was up, allowing the world to see his eyes, eyes that bulged with rage.

His name had once been Sergeant Nikolai Furin but for the last thirty-odd years he had been known by another name.

The Fury of Russia.

'Come and face me, children of my rival!' he bellowed at the front doors of the Pentagon. 'The Fury of Russia has arrived and with me the day of your doom!'

Cassie watched the TV in silence, her cell phone still pressed dumbly to her ear.

What will Green do? she wondered.

Will he come out—

On the television, a figure dressed in Army fatigues emerged on foot from the Pentagon.

His uniform was augmented with lime-green armoured plates on the shoulders and chest. His helmet had a custom-made green-tinted visor.

Clean-cut and handsome, with a square jaw and movie-star eyes, his face was known across America: he'd featured in television ads for military recruitment, including a famous one that had screened during the Superbowl.

And even though he was six feet tall, broad-shouldered and prodigiously fit, he looked tiny compared to the Fury.

'I'm here, asshole,' Cobalt Green said evenly.

GREEN

LOS ANGELES, CALIFORNIA
EIGHT YEARS AGO

Cassie sat in her modest kitchen with Cobalt Green, both of them sipping cheap instant coffee.

His olive t-shirt, emblazoned with the word ARMY, barely contained his bulging biceps. To the world he might have been Cobalt Green, but to Cassie he had always been her eldest brother, Greg.

'You always were the smartest of the lot of us,' he said.

'Black is way smarter than me,' Cassie said.

'He may be. He's also insane.' Greg scanned the little house and nodded approvingly. 'I like this place.'

That was a lie but at least it was a sweet one. The house was a small two-bedroom bungalow in a ratty street in L.A. not far from the 10 freeway.

Weeds sprouted in the drive. The concrete sidewalk out the front was cracked and buckled from numerous tiny quakes over the years. The house was painted beige but under the blazing southern California sun, the paint had faded. The furniture was plain and it bore all the usual household stuff, like a calendar on the fridge with some coloured Sharpies dangling from it.

'It's perfect for you,' he added.

'It's boring,' Cassie said.

'Inconspicuous.'

'It's ordinary.'

'It's you,' Greg said kindly.

Cassie nodded. He was right about that. 'Golden Gary wants to give the whole house a makeover, but the WITSEC people won't let him. Gotta fade into the background.'

'What we do is very public and that's never been you.'

'I'm sorry, Greg—'

'Don't be. Everyone needs home turf. Especially folks like us. This life of ours is a constant battle and the best place to fight a battle is on home turf.'

'I'm still sorry.'

'You had to do this. No matter what happens with the famous Cobalt, the rest of us will have things covered. And we all love our little sister.'

Cassie smiled, bowing her head. 'Thanks, Greg.'

Cobalt Green took in the quaint kitchen and nodded again.

'Like I said, you always were the smartest of us all.'

★ ★ ★

Cobalt Green was the pride of the U.S. Army, the soldier of soldiers. His skin was impenetrable, his strength unmatched, his leadership skills topnotch.

Perhaps most admirable of all, he had always submitted to the idea of rank: ascending to the rank of major through the regular process, saluting every officer who outranked him and obeying their commands, even though he could have killed them all in a second.

The Fury's first punch cracked his superstrong skull.

His second blow, to Green's lower back, broke his spine.

Then the Fury hurled Cobalt Green into the outer wall of the Pentagon.

A shocking impact.

Windows shattered.

Concrete pillars cracked.

Green fell to the grass beneath the wall and lay there slumped and moaning.

The Fury stomped over to him, grabbed his helmet and twisted it fiercely, wrenching Cobalt Green's head and part of his spinal column from his body.

A TV news crew captured the whole grisly encounter on film—a collection of fearful, running handheld images—and when it was all over, the Fury stood before their camera, holding up Cobalt Green's severed head, still wearing its helmet, the ragged skin at the throat dripping blood.

The shocking image made Cassie's blood run cold.

'Oh, Greg . . .' she whispered.

She could only imagine what the rest of America thought.

'He died on his knees!' the Fury bellowed. 'The green one! The poster child for your Army. Is he the best you can do, America?'

He threw Green's head to the ground and glared right down the lens of the camera.

'I am coming for you, children of Cobalt. I am coming to kill you all!'

And then he tore the Pentagon apart, storming through it, blasting through each of its concentric rings, destroying command centres and war-rooms and server farms and killing every officer and official he found.

When he was done, hundreds were dead and the gigantic five-sided building was left a smoking, broken ruin.

Then he flew north.

The children of Cobalt, Cassie thought.

There were eight of them in total: an elite group of heroes, each possessing superpowers like flight, strength, hearing and sight, but at only *half* the level of their mighty parent, Cobalt.

From birth they had been assigned military codenames: Green, Gold, Red, Purple, White, Silver and Black.

But because of a decision made ten years ago, the world was aware of only seven of them.

Cassie was the eighth.

And although she never used it, she had a codename, too.

Cobalt Blue.

Cassie swallowed deeply. How had it come to this?

For thirty years, international relations had existed in a state of balance if not exactly a state of peace and harmony.

In a state of Cold War.

Two rival superpowers, the United States and Russia, each with their own superhero.

But then the most unexpected thing happened, an event that had brought about this terrible day.

At the age of 79, the great American hero, Cobalt, had died of heart failure.

From: 'The Origins of the Super Cold War'
by Lynda Marren
(Extract from *The Atlantic* magazine)

THE JOINT MISSION

Ironically, it all started with an effort at peace: a joint U.S.–Russian space mission.

The old Cold War between the two superpowers, America and the U.S.S.R., had just ended and the Soviet Union was breaking apart.

Chaos reigned.

Breakaway republics claimed independence every week: Ukraine, Uzbekistan, Crimea, Georgia.

But Russia—always the central force behind the old Soviet Union—still had its nuclear arsenal and its space program, and in an effort to calm things, America and NASA proposed a joint mission to Venus.

Or, more precisely, to Venus's atmosphere.

★ ★ ★

A note about Venus.

Venus is unique in our solar system.

Its surface is a fiery hellscape with active volcanoes stretching to every horizon, constantly belching all manner of gaseous fumes into its atmosphere.

This makes that atmosphere a raging maelstrom of speeding winds, toxic gases, crushing pressure and exotic elements. It is hot, dense and nasty, entirely hostile to life.

It was this atmosphere with its unique elements that attracted Earth's two major powers.

America and Russia wanted to collect samples of those elements, so they joined forces for the fateful mission.

Heading the U.S. team for NASA was an astrophysicist named Dr Chris Cobalt.

INFECTED AND EMPOWERED

As everyone now knows, on its return to Earth, the Venus probe landed in the Arctic and was found by a team led by Dr Cobalt and a Russian special forces unit commanded by Sergeant Nikolai Furin.

Cobalt and Furin were standing right next to the probe when one of the satellite's superhot panels abruptly sprang open.

But something had attached itself to the probe's exterior—a tiny lifeform from the roiling atmosphere of Venus, no larger than a penny—and the sudden snapping open of the panel *broke the organism open* and from its tiny body sprang a cloud of strange gas that engulfed Cobalt's and Furin's faces.

Both collapsed instantly.

Both were then whisked away to secret, high-security containment facilities in their homelands.

And when, three months later, they both awoke, their DNA had been altered . . .

. . . and they had powers.

TWO SUPERHUMANS

The strength to lift an entire building.

High-frequency hearing.

The ability to see clearly for dozens of miles.

To hold their breath for over an hour.

To withstand a superheated blast.

And to fly at supersonic speed.

(The Fury was once clocked at Mach 2.1. He could chase down a fighter jet and outpace a commercial airliner.)

The thing was, Cobalt and Furin were perfectly matched, possessing exactly the same powers.

And thus a new Cold War began.

Cobalt chose a neutral uniform, sky-blue on white, with a small American flag on the shoulder.

The Russians resurrected an old symbol from their former days as a superpower: their hero wore dark red, with the yellow hammer and sickle of the old Soviet Union emblazoned on his chest and shoulder.

And he would take on a new name, one that suited the pent-up rage and frustration of an empire that had been humiliated and which would not be humiliated again.

INVASIONS AND AN UNSTABLE HERO

The new hero of Russia was the embodiment of terror.

He wasted no time restoring his country's wounded pride, one invasion at a time.

With the Fury at their head, Russian forces retook all the old Soviet republics.

And the Fury quickly showed that his brand of conquest was uncompromisingly pitiless.

He killed opposing troops when they surrendered.

He murdered the political leaders of beaten nations.

And he was particularly harsh on any resistance fighters he caught. He executed them—men, women, even children—by tearing their heads off in front of their loved ones. Then he killed those loved ones as well.

With his six-foot-six frame and deep-red hooded mask, his fearsome image became known across the world.

Sometimes he would remove the visor of his mask, revealing angry yellow-rimmed eyes.

It turned out that Sergeant Nikolai Furin was not a nice man to begin with.

His military records found their way to the American media and the story they told was unnerving.

Before entering the Russian Army at age 20, Furin had already been incarcerated twice, both times for hooligan-related violence.

Joining the Army, it turned out, had not been his choice: it was either that or another stint in prison.

Once in the Army, he'd been the subject of multiple disciplinary actions for disorderly conduct: fighting, insubordination—including *biting* a superior—plus three allegations of rape at three different training towns in outer Russia. All three charges had been dismissed when the women involved had all inexplicably died before they could testify.

Nikolai Furin had been 24 years old when he'd been infected, a volatile young man, barely in control.

And now he had unlimited power.

Russia didn't care.

The old K.G.B. agents who had elbowed their way into positions of power as their state had teetered on the brink of collapse now used him to further their own ambitions.

And the Russian people *loved* him.

They wore t-shirts with his face on them. Children played with Fury of Russia toys.

He was their hero.

Because he'd made their country a superpower again.

AMERICA'S HERO

Cobalt couldn't have been more different.

For one thing, Dr Chris Cobalt had been 44 at the time of their infection, twenty years older than Furin, and a highly respected astrophysicist. Where the Fury was all strength and rage, Cobalt was thoughtful and reserved. Curious about the extraterrestrial infection, Cobalt submitted to all manner of tests and physical examinations.

Cobalt wanted to learn, to know the cause and extent of these incredible new powers.

There was one other key difference between Cobalt and the Fury.

Dr Chris Cobalt was Dr *Christine* Cobalt. America's hero was a woman.

THE 'INVICIBLE PERSON' EXPERIMENT

And so the world got to watch, firsthand, a unique experiment: *If someone is invincible, if someone can do whatever they want without anyone to stop them, what will they do?*

Cobalt collaborated with the U.S. Government, the armed forces and NASA.

She lectured at universities, sharing what she had learned about herself.

She remained happily married to her husband, a bookish history professor named Arnold Cobalt. They had no children at the time she was infected.

Even when she became world famous—a superstar whose mere presence at an event would dwarf that of the President or any celebrity—she'd kept living for many years in the same modest home in north Texas she shared with her husband (until, of course, the notorious incident that had precipitated their move to Montana).

The Fury, on the other hand, did whatever he pleased.

If he admired a woman in a bar, he wouldn't hesitate

to kill her husband or boyfriend and just take her home with him.

He killed Russian Army officers who disagreed with him.

He once flew to his old boot camp in Siberia to murder a drill sergeant he felt had treated him poorly when he'd first joined the Army.

The Russian Government scrambled to placate him.

Mansions. Cars. Women.

Anything to calm his vicious temper and keep him content.

THE NEXT GENERATION

Naturally, during those heady times both America and Russia engaged in secret programs to create offspring from their superheroes.

They embarked on their programs immediately and in characteristically different ways.

The Russians put out a call for women to mate with the Fury.

Thousands volunteered.

Women from all over Russia converged on Moscow, hoping to be impregnated by the Fury.

The Fury loved it.

He had a voracious sexual appetite and he happily bedded six women a night. He reportedly killed twenty of them during the act.

Thirty-seven pregnancies resulted but ultimately—because of irregularities in his sperm or perhaps because only women with suitably strong ova could contain his seed—only six children were successfully born.

All were male.

And all had powers.

Although, interestingly, they had precisely *half* the powers of their father. Half his strength. Half his speed.

They were named after Soviet cities or regions:

The Fury of Moscow.

The Fury of Leningrad.

The Fury of Stalingrad.

The Fury of Sevastopol.

The Fury of Odessa.

The Fury of Kazan.

America tried a different method: they extracted some of Cobalt's eggs and, using the sperm of carefully selected males—men from the worlds of science or the military or professional sport—used I.V.F. and surrogacy to bring any offspring to term.

Seven viable offspring were produced over the next four years: five males and two females.

They received these codenames:

COBALT GREEN.

COBALT GOLD.

COBALT RED.

COBALT PURPLE and WHITE (the twins).

COBALT SILVER.

COBALT BLACK.

And then, a full seven years after her initial infection, in secret, at the age of 51, Cobalt did something no-one expected.

She gave birth to a natural child, born to her and her husband, Arnold.

Of course, eventually word got out about the birth but no-one outside of the other Cobalt children and a few key government officials knew this child's actual name.

It was only a slip of the tongue by an ambitious junior member of the House Intelligence Committee trying to show off during a hearing that inadvertently revealed to the world the eighth child's codename:

COBALT BLUE.

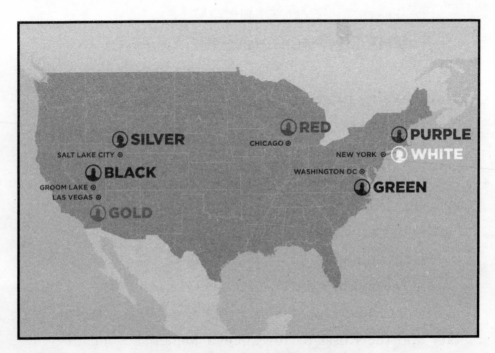

THE HEROES AND THEIR CITIES

CONCLUSION:
THE LOOMING AMERICAN FEAR

Three decades passed.

Flashpoints occurred, but in every instance Cobalt and the Fury defended their nations' interests and the precarious balance of *their* powers ensured a grudging peace between their two countries.

America prospered.

Russia did not.

And the children grew to adulthood.

The six Russian demi-heroes were forced into the military and the Russian Government kept them and their activities hidden.

In America, Cobalt's seven superchildren grew up together in a purpose-built home close to Cobalt's house in Texas. They didn't know it, but it was always under 24-hour armed military guard. And their skills and talents were monitored.

Up until their teens, they saw their mother almost every day for breakfast and dinner. She had insisted on that.

She wanted their childhoods to be as 'normal' as possible. They were, after all, half-brothers and sisters, and she wanted them to form the usual sibling relationships that siblings developed. As with all siblings, some became very close and others didn't.

Cobalt had also insisted that, as teenagers, they attend local public high schools. If they were going to grow up to be American superheroes, she reasoned, she wanted them to socialise with regular American kids and know their hopes and dreams. It'd also be good for them, she said.

And so it went until they all finished high school, at which point each of the seven superchildren were allowed to choose both their occupations and their home towns, and they took up a variety of roles in various cities.

Of course, they became instant celebrities, the heroes of their adopted cities.

Cobalt Green, the eldest, joined the U.S. Army and became a boon for enlistment.

Cobalt Gold, the second-oldest and the only homosexual of the litter, watched over Las Vegas and became a spokesman for gay and LGBTQ issues.

Cobalt Red joined the Chicago Police Department, insisting on going through the regular training program for new recruits.

The twins, Cobalts Purple and White, took up

residence in New York City, where they became fixtures on the social calendar, in between helping the N.Y.P.D. foil armed robberies.

Cobalt Silver lay low for her own reasons, reasons no-one readily knew. She lived quietly in Salt Lake City.

And then there was the troublesome Cobalt Black.

He did not have all the physical powers of his super-siblings, but that was not to say he wasn't powerful.

Due to his particular abilities, he experienced singular difficulties both at high school and afterward, so he was shifted out of public view to a military installation in Nevada.

Last of all, to this day, the eighth and youngest child, Cobalt Blue, remains a tantalising mystery, which only makes interested parties more curious about her, especially Russia. With its army of spies and internet farms, it is always trying to learn more about the last child of Cobalt, the natural one.

When all is said and done, however, a looming fear now hangs over America.

At the time they were infected, Cobalt was twenty years older than the Fury.

And despite their superhuman abilities, both have aged as regular humans do.

At the time of writing, Cobalt is 79 and will turn 80 this year. The Fury, on the other hand, is only 59, and still fit and healthy.

Cobalt will, in all likelihood, die of old age before the Fury does.

And when she does, it is only a question of how long the Russians and the Fury will wait to unleash their vengeance on America.

Cassie was still at her desk at J.P.L., staring in silent horror at her TV.

It was switching between images of the Fury holding the head of her half-brother Cobalt Green in one of his massive fists and the smoking ruins of the Pentagon.

A voice spoke in her ear.

'Cassie? Babe? You still there?'

Trey was still on the phone. She'd forgotten she was holding it.

'I'm here,' Cassie said flatly.

'You okay?'

'He waited one day. He came one day after the funeral.'

Trey said, 'This is gonna be a slaughter. On a national scale.'

Cassie stood up. 'I'm coming home.'

In the time it took for Cassie to drive home in L.A., the Fury of Russia flew from D.C. to New York City.

When he arrived there, he decapitated the Statue of Liberty—flew right through her neck—and impaled her head on top of One World Trade Center.

New Yorkers screamed in terror and fled the streets.

The Fury landed outside a trendy apartment building in SoHo. It was a well-known building, for it was the Manhattan residence of New York's heroes, the twins Cobalts Purple and White.

The Fury's voice boomed.

'I know this is where you live, Cobalt Purple and Cobalt White! Where you indulge in a life of play and frivolity. So I say again: COME AND FACE ME, CHILDREN OF MY RIVAL! THE FURY OF RUSSIA HAS ARRIVED AND WITH ME THE DAY OF YOUR DOOM!'

★ ★ ★

Inside that apartment building, two people dressed in superhero garb—one male, one female—stared down at the Russian behemoth.

'What do we do?' the woman, Cobalt White, gasped.

'Damn,' Cobalt Purple said.

■■■■■■■ PURPLE & WHITE ■■■■■■■

NEW YORK CITY
TWO YEARS AGO

Funky music played as Cassie sat on a plush velvet couch in Purple and White's ultra-cool New York pad.

Her handler at WITSEC, a no-nonsense U.S. Marshal by the name of Connie-Anne Walters, hadn't wanted her to visit her half-siblings in New York, but since Purple and White had a secret private elevator that ran direct to their heavily secured apartment, the Marshal had relented.

'Is this one of your songs, Winnie?' Cassie asked White.

Cobalt White—Winnie to family members—was 31 and jaw-droppingly beautiful, with spiked-up peroxide-blonde hair and gorgeous Eurasian features. Her and Purple's father had been an Asian American Army sniper whose sperm had connected with an egg donated by their mother.

In addition to her formal law-enforcement duties in New York City, White had done some modelling. She had also taken to DJ-ing lately and had been an instant hit. Every club wanted her to perform.

'Sure is,' she said. 'I love what you've done with your hair, Cassie.'

Cassie touched her hair self-consciously. It was plain mousy brown, totally unlike Winnie's electric white colouring, but she had cut it a little shorter during her last haircut.

'Thanks,' she said. 'Saw you in *Vanity Fair*. You looked amazing, especially in all those fight poses.'

'Annie Leibovitz did it. She can make anyone look amazing.'

That was White's modesty talking.

Modelling and DJ-ing aside, Cobalt White was mainly known for her incredible fighting skills. An expert in martial arts, she was a black belt in everything from karate and jiu-jitsu to kickboxing.

She was also more flexible than anyone Cassie had ever known. The ten-page *Vanity Fair* spread—plus the cover, of course—had shown her in a range of fight poses, her legs and arms extended at all kinds of extreme angles.

It had been the biggest-selling and most-downloaded issue of the year.

Cassie turned to White's twin brother, Purple. 'And

you, Paul. You're everywhere, too. So what is Cobalt Purple's secret to great abs?'

'Genetics,' Purple said with a grin.

He was also Asian American and wore his hair spiked up with gel, the tips coloured hot purple.

He was his sister's equal at martial arts. His disciplines were taekwondo and Krav Maga and he was so good, he'd been a judge at tournaments, including once at the Olympics for taekwondo.

Both twins wore form-fitting hero suits that allowed for maximum movement and that were accented with the colours of their codenames.

'What's tonight's party?' Cassie asked.

'Tonight's the pre-Met Gala,' Purple said. 'Tomorrow's the Gala. And after that's the afterparty which is always the best—'

At that moment, the back door burst open, and in walked someone Cassie could only describe as a joyous human whirlwind.

It was Cobalt Gold, a.k.a. Golden Gary.

With his thickly muscled arms and long bleached-blond hair that made him look like a 1980s rock drummer, he was big, loud and very, very gay.

Among all her superpowered siblings, he was Cassie's favourite.

Gary was the second-oldest of the eight of them, a few

months younger than Cobalt Green, yet he and Green couldn't have been more different.

Where Green was all measured and composed, the very embodiment of the Army values he treasured, Gary was flamboyance personified.

The two of them actually got along great—which was not always the case with the Cobalt children. Green and Red, for instance, often clashed, and everyone had trouble with the prickly Cobalt Black.

Friendly and gregarious as he was, Gary was not to be trifled with.

Perhaps in response to the inevitable anti-gay taunts he'd received as a teenager, he'd thrown himself into martial arts. It was he who, at the age of 13, had first instructed Purple and White, then both 10, in fighting skills, and he still coached them to this day.

That said, it should be mentioned that Cobalt Green and Golden Gary did have one singular thing in common.

They had both always—always—acted as fiercely protective older brothers to Cassie.

'Hey-ho, funsters!' Golden Gary called.

'Double G!' White squealed with delight.

'The Golden Gay Man from Vegas is in da house!' Purple shouted.

Purple threw some playful karate swings at Gary who, equally playfully, ducked them.

Then Gary dropped to one knee before the twins and said in a comical British accent, 'My noble brother, Knight of the Purple! My dear sister, Mistress of the White. It is so good to see you both!'

He turned to Cassie.

'And you. The most gorgeous one of all.' He smiled warmly and gently kissed her hand.

Cassie nodded. 'Hey, Gary. How're you doing?'

'In between keeping the streets of Vegas safe and being a gay icon? I'm gold, I'm gay and I'm fabulous. How 'bout you? How's that cute little boyfriend of yours?'

'I married him.'

'Wait. You what—!' Gary began.

White looked dismayed. 'Oh, Cassie, I love weddings!'

'It was just us and a judge,' Cassie said.

'Oh, girl,' Gary said. 'I woulda given you the bachelorette weekend to end all bachelorette weekends!'

'Witness Protection kinda frowns on those . . . and your famous superhero half-siblings coming to your wedding. They only let me come here because you guys have that elevator in the back.'

'Comes in handy,' White said.

Purple said, 'Your man's really smart, too, isn't he?'

Golden Gary answered for her. 'He's an aerospace engineer, dumbass, so yeah.'

Cassie said, 'Trey works at SpaceX. They collaborate with us a lot at J.P.L.'

'He's sweet,' White said. 'When I met him, I liked how he was always noting down his thoughts on his Voice Memos app.'

'That's Trey,' Cassie nodded. It was true, he loved the voice recording app, especially late at night in bed when he'd reach for his phone in the darkness and whisper some thought or idea into it. ('I always forget those ideas by morning and I hate doing that!' he'd say.)

'So he's literally a rocket scientist?' Purple asked.

Cassie nodded.

White said, 'And you're so clever, too. You two will have the smartest babies.'

'And you work hard, Cassie,' Purple added. 'You stick at things, more than we do, anyway. And I'm not a dumbass.'

'You so are,' Gary said.

'Shhh, you two!' White said. 'I like hearing about young engineers in love.'

'Thank you, Winnie,' Cassie said. 'Hey, not all of us can have our dating lives covered in the tabloids. Look at you all. This is what you were born for. Big. Loud. Heroes.'

She jerked her chin at Golden Gary.

'Especially you.'

'Oh, please. You'll make me blush,' he said impishly.

NEW YORK CITY
TODAY

High above Fifth Avenue, Cobalts White and Purple fought the Fury with every martial art skill they had.

It was a violent, fast and furious fight.

White unleashed a burst of spinning high kicks—while flying—at the same time as Purple shot down from above and unloaded a series of super-powerful punches at weak spots in the Fury's armour.

Bigger and more cumbersome than the twins, the Fury recoiled at their rapid-fire blows and practised coordination.

As the superfast rolling fight moved along the length of Fifth Avenue to the airspace in front of the New York Public Library, White even managed to dent the Fury's facemask and he sprang back in surprise.

The twins kept at it, harrying him, hitting him, moving with speed and cooperation, and just when it seemed that the two of them might overwhelm the Russian super-human, Cobalt White rushed down at him from above with her right leg poised. But he pivoted and she went by him and he reached out with one of his giant fists and snatched hold of her by the leg and the throat and—in a single, shocking instant—broke her neck like a twig and threw her like a rag doll toward the ground two hundred feet below.

Winnie smashed through one of the huge lion statues in front of the library, blasting it into pebbles.

She came to rest in front of the grand old building, lying face-down on its steps, her neck broken, unable to move and groaning in agony.

Seeing his sister fall, Purple redoubled his efforts, hurling blows at the Fury in the air.

But now the Fury's twofold advantages in strength and power began to show.

As their fight moved toward the Empire State Building further down Fifth, he just absorbed Purple's kicks and punches, barely even reacting, before abruptly he managed to get hold of Purple and hit him square in the face.

Purple's nose broke.

Blood sprayed.

His head was thrown back and his eyes rolled, so stunned was he by the power of the blow.

It was then that, gripping the limp body of Cobalt Purple, the Fury of Russia flew down the face of the Empire State Building at speed, *grinding* Purple's body against its windows, causing them to shatter in a long wave-like sequence of showering glass.

It finished with the Fury slamming Cobalt Purple into Fifth Avenue with such force that he created a crater in the middle of the street and sent hundreds of tiny missiles of rock fanning out in every direction.

But the colossal impact didn't kill Purple. He lay on the street, moaning, dazed.

So the Fury clenched one of his fists and punched him so hard in the face that the blow penetrated Purple's skull completely, breaking it open like a burst tomato.

That killed him.

A groaning sound made the Fury spin.

As he turned he yanked his bloody fist out of the remnants of Purple's head and saw Purple's twin sister, Cobalt White, still on the steps of the public library, gamely trying to move her arms, but because of her broken neck, completely unable to.

The Fury grabbed a nearby traffic light pole, snapped it in half and carried it over to Cobalt White.

He stabbed her through the back with it.

Cobalt White shuddered horribly before she went still, dead.

The Fury of Russia stood over the bodies of New York's superheroes and looked up at the city around him.

'I can smell your fear, America! I drink it in! I love it!'

Then he let out a primal roar of triumph.

LOS ANGELES

As Cassie turned onto her street in south L.A., a news-reader on her car radio said:

'*We are getting reports from New York that the Fury of Russia has killed both Cobalt Purple and Cobalt White...*'

Cassie pulled her car into the driveway of her little house and stopped.

She sat for a moment in the driver's seat. She thought about Purple and White—Paul and Winnie—their beautiful smiles and kind souls. She also pondered their formidable martial arts training, which against the Fury had evidently amounted to nothing.

Jesus Christ.

Cassie took a deep breath, regathered herself and raced inside.

Trey met her at the door.

'He just killed Winnie and Paul,' he said.

'I know.'

'With all their fighting skills, they didn't even . . .'

'I know,' Cassie said.

'What's gonna stop this guy? I mean, what does he want?' Trey asked.

Cassie looked hard at her husband. 'Mom told me. Couple weeks ago. When she was dying.'

■■■■ COBALT ■■■■

DILLON, MONTANA
TWO WEEKS AGO

They'd set up the hospital bed in Cobalt's bedroom, so the ailing hero could look out at the view she loved so much.

Out that window, she could see an almost endless panorama of Montana prairie, classic Big Sky country stretching for miles to the mountains.

Cobalt and her husband owned all that land, everything for sixty miles in every direction; in fact, their modest little ranch house was the only structure in the area.

The remote house and the land all around it had been bought for a reason: a previous unpleasant episode at their old place in north Texas.

Cassie sat beside the bed, holding her dying mother's hand.

Christine Cobalt was 79 but she looked older.

She'd aged terribly these past few months. The doctors who examined her—the best in the country—had said that her heart looked like that of a 100-year-old. It was literally worn out.

Flying across oceans, lifting trucks out of flooded rivers and diverting the lava flows of Hawaiian volcanoes—let alone deflecting bullets—had put such a strain on her heart that, a few months ago, it had started to beat out of rhythm.

Then it had started to fail.

'I was human before I was superhuman,' she said wryly to Cassie. Her voice was husky, pained, a shadow of its former self. 'For every action there is an equal and opposite reaction.'

Cassie snuffed a rueful laugh. 'I don't think Isaac Newton was thinking of superheroes when he came up with that concept. If you die, what will the Fury do? What does he want?'

Cobalt gazed absently out the window but she clearly wasn't seeing the view.

'He wants what every resentful psychopath with no boundaries and a lifetime of anti-American indoctrination has always wanted. He wants to storm America, kidnap the President and First Lady and rape her in front of him on national television. He wants to violate this country, traumatise it in front of the world every single day. And don't forget what he told me at the summit in Paris about what he wants to do to you, if he can find you.'

Cassie gulped. 'Yeah.'

'And after I die, there will be no-one to stop him,' Christine Cobalt said.

'Red could do it. Green, too,' Cassie said hopefully.

'No. Since only half their genes come from me, they have only half my powers. Half as strong. Half as fast.'

Cassie said, 'What about together?'

'Even then . . .'

'There has to be a way to kill him,' Cassie said. 'A weakness.'

'Oh, he has a weakness. Same as mine,' Cobalt said. 'His skin may be an invulnerable polymer and his bones harder than any alloy, but he was also human before he was superhuman.'

'Meaning?'

'His heart and internal organs are strong, but not as strong as his outer skin. Look at me. Being a hero over-worked my heart and now I'm screwed.'

'He still needs to breathe . . .' Cassie said thoughtfully.

'Correct. To fly at altitude, for instance, he needs the mask for oxygen.'

'So he can drown?'

'In theory.'

'And suffocate?' Cassie asked.

'Yes. But then he can also hold his breath for an hour. And who besides me can hold him underwater for that long?'

'So his mask is also protective?'

'Yes. But again, who besides me could get close enough to him to rip it off and get a super-powerful grenade of some kind down his throat? We thought about trying something like that in Paris when I shook his hand, but we decided that if I failed, he'd level western Europe.'

'Does Black have any ideas?' Cassie asked.

A short pause followed, as often happened when Cobalt Black's name was mentioned.

'Of course,' her mother said. 'He suggested setting a trap. Pick a city, ring it with ten thermonuclear weapons, and blow up the Fury and the city when he arrives.'

'With the citizens *still there*?' Cassie said incredulously.

'Yes. Black doesn't think the way you or I do, unburdened as he is by pesky things like a conscience.' Cobalt turned to face her daughter directly. 'So how's anonymity?'

'It's good,' Cassie said. 'I'm not like the others.'

'In your own way, you are.'

'I'm fast but only kinda strong—'

'You're smart,' Cobalt said firmly. 'The others, they

all got strength and flight and that stuff, but you got the brains.'

'No, Black got all the brainpower—'

'Too much of it,' Cobalt said. 'You could still come out and be Cobalt Blue.'

The comment came with a meaningful look.

'You and Dad always said it was my choice,' Cassie said softly.

'And it still is,' Cobalt replied. 'But I *am* still allowed to nudge you in another direction, try to convince you otherwise.'

Cassie looked away.

'I anticipated what the modern world would do to us,' she said.

'And that was?'

'Turn us into celebrities!' Cassie exclaimed. 'Cereal boxes. Invites to the Oscars. I knew the modern world would turn us into human trophies and it did! That's okay for White and Purple and Gold, they love all that, but it's not for me!'

The great Cobalt stared back at her daughter.

'And that's precisely your power,' she said evenly. 'You can imagine the future. Plan for it. I can't do that. Your brothers and sisters can't do that.'

She fell back against her pillows and sighed deeply. 'Cassie. I once met the parents of a kid with severe mental disabilities. They were in their seventies *and they were petrified*. They were petrified of dying, because they didn't know what would happen to their kid after they were gone. That's how I feel now. A terrifying future is coming and I won't be here.'

Cassie said nothing.

'The Fury of Russia,' Cobalt went on, 'can't be beaten with strength or speed or flight. Only smarts. Which means, in the end, whether you like it or not—'

The hero looked her natural-born daughter squarely in the eye.

'—it'll come down to you.'

LOS ANGELES
TODAY

Cassie's cell phone rang, loud and sudden. The caller ID read: RED.

Cassie answered it. 'Reggie.'

'ATAC got a satellite fix on him. He's on his way here from New York. After taking care of the east coast, it looks like he's working his way across the country. I'm next. Then it'll be Silvia, Gary, Blaine—'

This was typical of Reggie, Cobalt Red.

Straight to business. No small talk. No wonder he'd never got along with White and Purple and, sadly, Cobalt Green.

'Oh, Reggie . . .' Cassie said.

'—then you. If he can find you.'

'Where are you now?' Cassie asked.

★ ★ ★

Cobalt Red stood inside City Hall in his home town of Chicago.

He was outside the mayor's office, having just had a meeting with the city's senior officials.

'The mayor wants me to leave Chicago,' he said flatly into his phone.

'What!' Cassie said.

'To "minimise damage" in the event that I lose.'

'Are you kidding me?'

Red shook his head. 'They're already planning for life after. I *protected* this city, these people, for twelve years, and now they want me out of here so their windows don't get broken when he comes to kill me.'

'That's just . . .'

Red said, 'You were smart. You laid low, lived out of sight.'

'Reggie . . .'

Red shook his head. 'I have to admit, I enjoyed it, Cassie. Bit of limelight. Good tables at restaurants. I haven't had to pay for a drink in a bar in years. But now—'

Cassie whispered to herself, 'It all means nothing.'

'—it all means nothing,' Red said, even though he hadn't heard her. 'Now they don't want to know me!'

'They're scared.'

'I didn't want to be like Purple and White: celebrity superheroes,' Red vented. 'Or Gary in Vegas, pushing his agendas. Or Green, the Army's super-soldier working out of the Pentagon. Or Black, doing whatever the hell he does in his lab. I kept it low-key as a cop. Reduced gun crime, helped inner-city kids. They still made me into a hero, a goddamned tourist stop.'

He took a breath. 'You said this would happen.'

'Yeah . . .' Cassie said.

'I never really got why you chose Witness Protection but I get it now,' Red said.

'I wanted my life to be mine.'

'You always were the smartest of us all.'

'What're you going to do?' Cassie asked.

'I'm going to fight him is what I'm going to do,' Red said bitterly. 'North of town, out over the lake. Keep their precious city intact. And I'm probably gonna lose.'

'Don't say that, Reggie.'

'I'm sorry, Cassie.'

'What for?'

'For not being more understanding when you made your decision. For not getting it back then. You were right. You were the only one who—'

A sudden sonic boom above the city made Red spin and look out the window.

'He's here. Sorry, Cassie, I gotta go now. See you on the other side.'

And he hung up.

▰▰▰▰▰▰▰ RED ▰▰▰▰▰▰▰

NORTH TEXAS
TWELVE YEARS AGO

Cassie was 17. Red was 22.

They were in the basement of Cassie's parents' home in north Texas. It was early morning.

They both wore simple gym clothes: her top had the name of the local high school on it, his read C.P.D.

'Okay, today we begin your fight training,' Red said. 'Now, Golden Gary, he can teach you all kinds of pretty techniques and flashy moves, but I'm gonna teach you something else. I'm gonna teach you *how* people fight.'

'All right,' Cassie said.

'First thing,' Cobalt Red said, 'is knowing when a fight has started. We've all been brought up with the notion of "They threw the first punch. I just defended myself." Now, this kind of thinking seems noble and all, but it has flaws, not least because it presupposes that you can win a fight *starting from behind*, after you've already been hit. America beat the Japanese in World War II *after* they bombed us at Pearl Harbor. We took a hit, came back, and won. All very noble and honourable.'

'Right,' Cassie said.

Red shook his head. 'Wrong. Nope, there are times when you gotta realise *that the fight has already started* and you'll need to throw the first punch. When a big dude in a bar comes lumbering toward you, bunching his fists, trust me, the fight has already started.'

Cassie nodded.

This had actually been an issue for Red, indeed for several of the Cobalt males: cocky men in bars—sometimes groups of them—wanting to test a Cobalt in a fight, to see if they really were super.

'Right then, hit me,' Cobalt Red said.

She swung at him.

He ducked.

She missed.

'I said hit me!'

Another swing. Another swerve. Another miss.

'Come on! You can do better than that! HIT ME!'

Cassie was pissed now, so she unleashed a flurry of blows . . .

. . . but Red dodged all of them.

On the last swing, he stepped nimbly behind a punching bag and casually swung it into her, knocking Cassie onto her ass.

But Cassie wasn't done.

Ever determined, she got up—only to be punched hard in the nose by Red.

She dropped like a sack of shit, clutching her face.

'Ow!'

'Everyone should get punched in the face once in their lives,' Red said.

'Why?' Cassie didn't think so right then.

'Because,' Red said, 'in that moment of dizziness, your heart races and the mere idea of another punch sends your mind into fight or flight mode.'

'You mean resilience?'

'I mean: to know you can take a punch and keep going. When someone hits you, you get dizzy, your vision blurs, but can you still *think* clearly?'

'So what's the key?'

'If you get hit in a fight, you gotta keep your wits long enough to avoid the killer blow that's comin' in next. Till then, don't get hit.'

'So how do I duck a punch?'

'By watching. Hit me.'

She wound up to strike him.

'Okay, hold it there,' Red said.

She froze with her right fist pulled back.

'So here's what I see,' Red said. 'You're winding up for a cross. All your weight is loaded back to the right. So I'm ducking left. Punch.'

She swung. He ducked left . . . so she missed.

'That's the key. *Watch*. Watch where your attacker

loads up and you'll know where he's going. Read the punch before it comes.'

They fought some more.

Now Red swung at Cassie. She ducked left. The blow missed.

More punches. More ducking. She got hit a few times, fell onto her ass again.

Got up.

Bobbed down. Miss.

Bobbed and swerved. Miss. Miss.

By this time, she was drenched in sweat.

'Now block me!' Red called.

She parried his blows.

Red yelled, 'I don't care if you're tired! Your attacker won't! Now, duck, bob and hit.'

She ducked, bobbed up and landed a solid punch right in Red's face.

And this time he ended up on his ass. He grinned, impressed.

'Nice hit, little sister.'

Cassie staggered over to a bench, sat down heavily and wrapped a towel around her neck, exhausted.

Red sat beside her, patted her on the shoulder. 'That was a good session. Nice work.'

He rubbed his jaw.

'That really was a solid hit.' He stood to go. 'Same

time tomorrow?'

'What?!'

'This is an expression of my love for you,' Cobalt Red said.

As she remembered those training sessions, Cassie thought about Red.

He'd never been good at softening the way he spoke, at giving news gently.

It was why he'd never got along with Green. Greg could play the game, especially the Army game at the Pentagon.

Red couldn't. He was simply unable to do it. He was hardwired differently: he was too literal, too plain-spoken, too blunt.

But he'd been telling the truth: those sessions really were an expression of his love.

LAKE MICHIGAN, NORTH OF CHICAGO
TODAY

In the sky above Lake Michigan, the Fury of Russia battled Cobalt Red.

It was a bare-knuckle street fight in the air: both flew in sweeping arcs over the lake, pivoting to unleash big savage punches or powerful elbow blows.

Red fought doggedly, determinedly.

He wasn't a classically trained martial arts fighter like Cobalts Gold, White and Purple.

He was a scrapper, plucky, the kind of fighting man whose skills were functional, utilitarian, ugly, honed on the street to take down thugs and criminals.

Not unlike the Fury.

But with half the speed and half the strength of his opponent, Red had to go for hard and powerful strikes and he landed many until—

Wham.

—the Fury anticipated his next move and Red ran face-first into a fist that felt like pure iron.

His ears rang. He felt dizzy.

He almost lost consciousness and dropped out of the sky, bringing himself into a hover just above the water.

He shook it off, trying desperately to keep his wits, just as he'd instructed Cassie, so he could avoid the killer blow that would most assuredly be coming in next—

It came.

It was the most dreadful of blows, simply horrific, a punch of such shocking intensity that it broke Red's jaw—already far stronger than the average human jaw— in four places.

Red was hurled across the lake so hard he skimmed across its surface and ran up onto the shore, gouging a trench eighty yards long up the beach.

He lay still.

His eyes stared up at the sky but they saw nothing.

Cobalt Red was dead.

The punch had killed him.

The Fury of Russia landed on the sand beside him.

'You fought well, policeman,' he said. 'With grit and with courage and heart. This was a good death. Pity no-one from your city was here to witness it.'

★ ★ ★

Over the next half-hour, the Fury proceeded to topple every building on Lake Shore Drive. Then, in a tremendous display of strength, he lifted the Hancock Tower from its foundations and dropped it on Wrigley Field, crushing the century-old baseball stadium.

After that, he lifted the city's tallest skyscraper, Willis Tower, out of the ground and tossed it onto Soldier Field—the home ground of the Chicago Bears football team, but perhaps more importantly, a stadium named in honour of American soldiers who had fought in World War I and which had been the venue for massive support-the-war-effort rallies during World War II.

With the city of Chicago in ruins, the Fury calmly flew off, heading west.

LOS ANGELES
TODAY

The news of Red's death came through social media first, then on the radio and TV.

He'd been killed by the Fury on the northern outskirts of Chicago.

Cassie and Trey both listened to the report in silence.

Cassie thought of her plainspoken half-brother who, when he could have become anything, had chosen to become a Chicago cop. However socially awkward he might have been, he'd always been genuine. It had made him a great cop and an honest brother. And now he was gone.

'That's four in the space of a morning,' Cassie said. 'Only four of us left now: Silvy, Gary, Blaine and me.'

'Where do they keep Black now?' Trey asked.

'Nevada. At the Groom Lake complex.'

'In a padded cell?'

'A secure lab, at least that's what the military call it. They say that the Fury's fourth son, the Fury of Sevastopol, is also a genius who the Russians keep out of sight,' Cassie said.

'Is he psychotic, too?' Trey said.

'Black's brain is supercharged but the human brain wasn't designed to hold that many thoughts.'

'When was the last time you saw him?'

Cassie said, 'About a year ago. When he said this would happen.'

BLACK

GROOM LAKE MILITARY TESTING COMPLEX (RESTRICTED ACCESS), NEVADA
ONE YEAR AGO

Christine Cobalt was waiting in a sweltering-hot parking lot in the Nevada desert when Cassie pulled up in her beat-up Jeep.

Cassie wore a cap, sunglasses and a buff around her nose and mouth so that the guards wouldn't see her face. They were at a heavily guarded military facility about forty miles outside Vegas.

Next to the great Cobalt was her husband and

Cassie's father, Professor Arnold Cobalt.

Arnie Cobalt had a horseshoe of hair around his otherwise bald head, bright curious eyes and an expressive face that was almost always smiling.

He sat in a wheelchair—as he had ever since the incident at their old north Texas home—but as usual, his spirits were high.

'Hey there, kiddo!' he said to Cassie.

Cassie hugged him warmly. 'Hey, Dad.'

Her mother said, 'He asked for you and me, but I wanted to bring your dad, too.'

'Why me?' Cassie said.

Her interactions with Black had been minimal over the years and for good reason.

Black was brilliant, sure, but also volatile and prone to nasty psychological attacks on his super half-siblings. It was thought best to keep Cassie away from him as much as possible.

'Who knows how his mind works?' Christine Cobalt said.

They headed inside the nearest building, passing four U.S. Army guards flanking the doors.

They met Cobalt Black inside his secure lab.

It had a dozen computers, countertops with

chemistry equipment, whiteboards, blackboards, even a miniature wind-tunnel that he had requested, all of it contained behind a heavy steel blast door.

The blast door had ostensibly been designed to keep Cobalt Black and his remarkable brain safe from Russian kidnappers, although many said in hushed whispers that it had also been designed to keep Black *in*.

Cobalt Black paced behind one of his countertops. He rarely kept still. Rarely stopped muttering.

He was 30 years old, the second-youngest of the Cobalt children, and had long black straggly hair and wild eyes. His face was shot through with creases: worry marks caused by constant thinking and frowning.

Unlike his brothers, Red, Green, Purple and Golden Gary, he was not naturally muscular. He was lean and gangly, to the point of looking malnourished.

But that was not to say he didn't have powers. Thin as he was, he was still strong, had enhanced hearing and smell, and could fly short distances.

His chief super ability, though, was mental.

He had an IQ of 275: a number that was literally off the charts.

Cobalt Black was smart. Really smart.

Too smart.

★ ★ ★

Cassie and her parents sat in Black's high-tech lab.

Cassie noticed that even her mother, her powerful mother, was watching Black uncertainly. She was on edge, perhaps even afraid.

'Hello, Mother,' Cobalt Black said brightly, 'you look like shit. How long have you got?'

'Doctors say a year.'

'I give you nine months, tops. Your body's been writing cheques that your heart could never pay. And when you're dead, he's gonna come here and rip this country a new asshole.'

'Now, Blaine—' Cassie's dad said.

Black's eyes flashed. 'I'm sorry. What powers have *you* got again? Wheelchair-pushing ones? His boys took care of you without breaking a sweat, so you don't get to contribute, old man.'

'Blaine. Manners,' Christine Cobalt said.

Black stepped back, bowed his head. 'Right. Yeah. Sorry, sorry. Gotta treat the lesser mortals with respect.'

Seeing him retreat, Cassie's eyes suddenly narrowed.

'Where are you, Blaine?' she asked. It was a curious question and her parents frowned at it, not understanding.

But Black got it.

A reptilian grin spread across his face.

'You *are* clever,' he said.

Cassie stood, walked over to Black *and waved her hand through his body.*

Cobalt Black wasn't there.

He was a hologram: a perfectly realistic hologram.

Cassie spotted a small silver disc sitting on the floor below the hologram, emitting the image. It had been out of sight, behind the countertop.

At that moment, the hologram winked out and a figure appeared behind Cassie and her parents, standing in the doorway to the lab: the real Cobalt Black.

He wore the same clothes as his hologram had. His eyes, Cassie saw, were still definitely crazy.

'How did you know?' he asked.

Cassie said, 'I saw a flicker at your fingertips when you moved. You musta stepped outside the 3D camera.'

'You're the first one to spot it.'

'I'm honoured.'

'Dear sister, I have an IQ of 275. Yours is 140. There is nothing you can think of that I haven't thought of first. I didn't step out of the camera's range unintentionally: I've done it every time I've used my display. It was a clue that only you saw.'

As she stood in front of him, Cassie poked Black in the chest, just to be sure that he was real. He was.

'Is that why you brought me here? To test me?' she asked.

'To prepare you. For when she dies.' He jerked his chin at their mother.

'Meaning?'

'Leave. Because he'll find you. He's very predictable, this Fury. He's not just going to destroy this country, he's going to eviscerate it, crush its monuments, murder its people, and piss on everything it holds dear. But he'll save the worst for us, the children of Cobalt, especially you, the only one born out of love, not a test tube.'

Christine Cobalt said, 'You're the smartest guy in America, Blaine. Can't you think of any way to beat him?'

'I told you my plan, Mother—'

'Other than blowing up an entire American city and its citizens with a nuclear warhead.'

'Ten warheads. Ten. One isn't enough, but ten should do it.'

'What about the innocent civilians?' Cassie said.

'An acceptable sacrifice. He won't believe we'd do such a terrible thing.'

'Other than that,' Christine Cobalt said.

'Then no,' Black said.

Cassie said, 'There has to be a way—'

'There isn't,' Black said. 'It's simple math.'

Cassie shook her head. 'How can you be so . . . *emotionless*?'

Black's eyes were blank. 'The most successful species on this planet—crocodiles and sharks—dispensed with emotion millions of years ago because it is an evolutionary handicap. Here are the facts: when she dies, the ultimate apex predator will come to this country. He will kill her children one by one and then he will install himself as a sadistic tyrant.'

'Then we have to think of something—'

'It's *math*,' Black declared again. 'In the absence of our mother, the Fury will be unstoppable. As I said, I brought you here to give you the best advice you'll ever get: leave before he arrives.'

Back in their kitchen, Trey said, 'That's what America's greatest mind said? That the Fury is unbeatable and unstoppable?'

Cassie said, 'Whatever his other flaws, you'll always get the truth from Black. Planes, missiles, they're all useless against the Fury. And now he's here, moving steadily westward, heading this way.'

'Hey,' Trey said. 'Remember, you and your dad once beat two of his asshole sons when they came to kill you.'

Cassie looked hard at her husband, remembering that terrible night.

I THE ASSASSINATION ATTEMPT
I

NORTH TEXAS
TEN YEARS AGO

It was the night of the hundred-year storm. The rain fell in lashing sheets.

Lightning flashed. Thunder boomed.

And Cassie and her father, Professor Arnold Cobalt, were huddled behind the counter in their kitchen, fearfully watching the two hulking figures standing outside the kitchen's glass doors, in the rain, peering in, searching for them.

They had floated down silently from the sky moments earlier, flying under their own power.

The Fury of Odessa and the Fury of Kazan: the Fury's two youngest sons.

Here. Now. On American soil.

They were huge specimens: well over six feet tall and bulky, like linebackers, with thick necks and massive shoulders. And they both had overly wide yellow-rimmed eyes, just like their father.

Cassie was 19, her father 69. Arnold Cobalt was a small, sweet man entirely devoid of athletic ability. But he was the most popular history professor at the local university.

'How did they get this far into the country?' Cassie whispered.

Arnold Cobalt and his famous wife lived about thirty miles north of Amarillo, right in the middle of the Texas Panhandle in the far north of the state, over six hundred miles from the Gulf.

'I don't know—' her dad replied.

Cassie grabbed his arm and yanked him across a short gap of open space, crouch-running quickly out of the kitchen just as one of the two Russian superthugs broke the door down.

As Cassie and her dad came into the entry vestibule of the house, Arnie Cobalt pulled out his cell phone and hastily texted to 'Mom': *911 HOME.*

Cassie dragged him up the stairs—

—just as the Fury of Odessa emerged from the kitchen, dripping wet and calling, 'Come out, Professor Cobalt! And your pretty daughter, too!'

They fled into her bedroom upstairs. It had a window that opened onto the garage roof. Maybe, Cassie thought, they could get out that way.

Cassie threw open the window—

—to see the Fury of Kazan hovering outside it, the rain hammering down on his head, smiling nastily.

'Hello,' he said.

'Goodbye,' another voice said from behind them and Cassie spun to see the other one, the Fury of Odessa, standing in the doorway of the bedroom, blocking the exit that way.

They were trapped.

'At long last, we lay eyes on you,' Odessa said. 'The natural daughter of Cobalt. They hid you well. Our intelligence agencies know so little about you. My, you are pretty. Bet you're tasty, too.'

Kazan said, 'We thought we would give your heads to our father as a birthday gift.'

He took a step into the bedroom.

He assessed Arnie Cobalt and snorted. 'Look at you, puny man. Hard to know what the great Cobalt sees in you.'

In reply, Arnie snatched up a baseball bat from the floor and slammed it into Odessa's head.

The bat broke in two.

Odessa just blinked, completely unhurt.

Arnie said, 'Damn.'

Odessa said, 'I think I will knock out all of your teeth first. Then I will break your fingers one by one.'

He lunged at Arnie, swinging one of his huge fists—

—only to have the punch blocked.

By Cassie.

At first, the Fury of Odessa reeled in shock, then his face lit up, impressed.

'So. You have strength. But your father has none and there are two of us.'

Quick as a whip, he swung at Cassie but—just as Red had taught her—she ducked then bobbed and replied with a stinging punch right to his face, dropping the Fury of Odessa.

Then she grabbed her dad's hand and fled past Odessa back into the house.

They scampered down the carpeted stairs, with Arnie in the lead. He reached the bottom when abruptly, the Fury of Kazan appeared, flying in from outside, and grabbed Arnie.

Cassie halted halfway down the stairs.

The Fury of Kazan now stood at the bottom of the stairs, gripping her dad.

Then the Fury of Odessa appeared at the top of the staircase, rubbing his nose.

She was trapped again and now they had her father.

Kazan growled: 'One more step and I snap his spine.'

Cassie stood frozen on the stairs.

Kazan shrugged. 'I think I will snap his spine anyway.'

And with those horrific words, he punched Arnold Cobalt in his lower back and a sickening cracking noise was heard. Arnie's eyes bulged as he collapsed to the floor, crying out in agony.

'Dad!' Cassie yelled.

The Fury of Kazan glared up at her. 'Now, we have our way with you. Then we take both your heads.'

He took a step up.

His half-brother, the Fury of Odessa, still covered the top of the stairs.

Arnie Cobalt tried to crawl to his daughter's aid.

'No, you bastards!' he shouted.

Caught between the two Russian superthugs, Cassie didn't know what to do. She pressed herself against the wall.

Her father kept trying to crawl to her, to save her, but his legs were useless. 'Get away from her!'

At the top of the stairs, the Fury of Odessa ogled Cassie's body. 'I'm sure you taste very nice indeed . . .'

Whoosh!

The Fury of Odessa was suddenly swept out of sight.

One second he was there, the next he was gone. Just gone.

'Shit,' Kazan gasped. 'She's here . . .'

A moment later, another figure stood in Odessa's place at the top of the stairs.

Cobalt.

In full hero uniform.

In full hero stance: boots spread wide, fists on hips. And anger in her eyes.

'You came here to kill my family?' she asked.

'No, no . . . we . . .' the Fury of Kazan stammered.

'You came here to kill my family.' This time it wasn't a question.

'Fuck,' the Fury of Kazan said flatly.

They would be the last words he'd ever speak.

The next day, the severed heads of the two junior Furies were delivered to the Russian embassy in Washington, D.C., with a Post-it note that read:

RETURN TO SENDER

LOS ANGELES
TODAY

'We didn't beat them,' Cassie said. 'We just stayed alive long enough till Mom got there.'

'Still . . .' Trey said.

'Dad never walked again. And Mom never forgave the Russians. She got even madder at them after that whole cruise ship thing that occurred about six months after the Texas incident.'

'The cruise ship thing?' Trey said. 'You mean when she and Cobalt Green saved that liner—what was it called, the *Caribbean Sun* or something—from sinking off the Bahamas?'

Cassie nodded. 'It was called the *Caribbean Star* and it didn't just sink. There was a whole lot more to the incident than that.'

'What do you mean?'

'Mom and Green were wearing body cameras that

day and when she came back after, Mom showed me the footage from them,' Cassie said.

THE SINKING OF THE CARIBBEAN STAR

ATLANTIC OCEAN
THIRTY NAUTICAL MILES EAST OF THE BAHAMAS
NINE YEARS AGO

By the time Cobalt and her eldest son, Cobalt Green, arrived in the air above the stricken cruise ship, it was already half sunk, listing to one side, and going down fast.

The *Caribbean Star* was one of the largest cruise liners in the world.

Painted brilliant white and dotted with hundreds of blue-tinted windows, it was as tall as a forty-storey building and over a thousand feet long. It had a gross tonnage of 200,000 tons and carried 6,000 passengers and almost as many crew.

And right now the gigantic white boat was dramatically tilted over onto its port side, its lowest open deck about to go under.

Screams cut the air.

Passengers were leaping from the cruise liner, desperate to get off it before it went down.

Several dozen lifeboats had managed to get clear, but it had all happened so quickly that the lifeboats on the port side had all been submerged before they could be loaded with passengers and released.

Which meant half the souls on board the giant sinking ship had no ready means of escape.

'We have to stabilise her before that deck goes under!' Cobalt shouted to Green as they flew in toward it. 'Once that deck is flooded, the whole thing will sink like a stone! I figure we have about a minute. I'll take care of the ship. You help the passengers in the water: grab some lifeboats still attached to the submerged port side, bring them out and get them over to those people.'

'Got it!' Green called back.

They flew down through the sky, racing to the rescue.

Once at the ship, they worked fast.

Green flew straight underwater and brought up two lifeboats.

While he did that, the great Cobalt also blasted under the surface, zooming deeper, all the way beneath the ship, arriving at the mid-point of its hull where she—

—paused.

Cobalt squinted, seeing something in the gloom far

beneath her, something dark and metallic and moving away.

A submarine? she thought.

She had to let it go for now. She had lives to save and maybe thirty more seconds to save them.

She grabbed hold of the hull with both hands.

And then, in an astonishing display of her strength, she began to fly up, pushing upward . . .

. . . *lifting the entire ship out of the water!*

It was an incredible sight.

The great white cruise liner rose up and out of the ocean . . . and kept rising . . . until it was hovering in the air above the waves, hundreds of seawater waterfalls pouring off it, and there, underneath the massive thing, was the tiny figure of Cobalt, lifting it.

The passengers in the lifeboats cheered.

The emergence of the *Caribbean Star* from the water revealed its hull . . .

. . . and about seven or eight gaping holes below its waterline. They were all about six feet in diameter. The steel around some of these holes was bent *inward*, while the edges of others were bent outward.

It was as if a missile or torpedo of some kind had smashed *into* the hull and then smashed *out* of it, *several times*.

As Cobalt Green watched his mother raise the huge

ship out of the ocean and slowly begin the thirty-mile journey to land, he heard desperate shouts from inside it.

He flew quickly toward them.

Inside the now-flying ship, Green grabbed those passengers who had not been able to make it to a life-boat, or to leap off the cruise liner, in time. Many were elderly or infirm.

He shuttled them out, flying them to lifeboats and then racing back in again.

And then, as he followed the sounds of a woman's desperate screams, he swept into a stateroom on the first class deck . . .

. . . to see a grey-haired older man and an elderly woman kneeling on the floor while a tall figure dressed all in red stood ominously over them.

Green saw the tall red figure grip the kneeling man's neck in a headlock and rip his head clean off, spraying blood everywhere, while the woman screamed in terror.

'What the hell?' Green yelled.

The figure in red spun and the two locked eyes.

Green was stunned.

He'd never actually met one of them before, one of the Fury's supersons. He'd seen pictures, of course, surveil-lance photos, spy shots. But never had he encountered one in the flesh, up close.

And he'd seen enough pictures of this one to know

which son of the Fury he was: this was the eldest of the Fury's supersons, known as the Fury of Moscow.

The Fury of Moscow smiled at Cobalt Green.

He was actually quite handsome, with a lean face, pale skin and high cheekbones.

His eyes were eerie and yellow rimmed, and they didn't seem to blink, which made his smile all the more sinister.

When he spoke it was in English but the accent was pure Russian.

'Why, hello there,' he said. 'I did not think you would get here so quickly. I am so sorry you had to witness this. You were not supposed to.'

'What *the fuck* are you doing?' Green demanded.

Moscow shrugged at the slumped headless body at his feet.

'My family had some unfinished business with Secretary Kolhoffer here and I came to finish it.'

And with those words, the Fury of Moscow flew out through the window, shattering it, before diving straight down into the ocean and disappearing into its depths.

Cobalt Green thought about following him, but he had people to save, not least the sobbing elderly woman right in front of him, the wife of the former U.S. Secretary of Defence, Harold Kolhoffer.

★ ★ ★

It was later determined that the whole incident—the sinking of the *Caribbean Star*, the puncture holes created by the Fury of Moscow, who had crept up on the cruise liner on a Russian submarine—was meant as cover for the assassination of Kolhoffer, the highly regarded yet long-retired former Secretary of Defence who in his prime had been one of America's greatest statesmen.

With his quick wit and sharp retorts, he had been America's representative at several U.S.–Russia summits— the small ones before the famous summit in Paris—at which he had consistently made the Fury of Russia look like a fool.

It was those humiliations, it seemed, that had to be avenged.

The Fury of Moscow escaped on the submarine Cobalt had glimpsed earlier.

By the time Cobalt had safely returned the cruise ship to dry land and zoomed back out to the sinking site, the sub was nowhere to be found, presumably having gone deep, hiding in the darkness of the ocean floor where not even Cobalt could find it.

'I saw Greg's body-cam footage of that stateroom,' Cassie said. 'It was the most horrific thing I've ever seen. I also saw his exchange with the Fury of Moscow.'

Trey said, 'I've only ever seen the Fury's supersons at Russian military events on TV. What was he like?'

'Dangerous,' Cassie said. 'Psychotic, sure, but also cool and calm, in control, totally aware of what he was doing. Not on the edge of exploding with rage like his father.'

At that moment, the excited voice of a newsreader on the radio cut her off.

'The President has just released a statement from his secret location. It reads: "I am horrified and appalled by these attacks on our sovereignty by the Fury of Russia. It is in flagrant violation of the peace accords that were agreed upon at the Paris summit eight years ago."'

Cassie bit her lip in thought. 'The summit . . .' she said softly.

■■■■■ THE PARIS SUMMIT ■■■■■

PARIS, FRANCE
EIGHT YEARS AGO

It was, the television pundits agreed, the greatest meeting of all time.

The two superheroes of the two superpowers in the same room, on neutral ground, coming together to sort out their countries' differences.

In the grand ballroom of the Palace of Versailles, Cobalt and the Fury stood on a podium in front of two hundred journalists from around the world.

Cameras flashed.

TV cameras filmed.

Behind Cobalt was the American flag.

Behind the Fury was the Russian flag.

At Cobalt's side was the U.S. Secretary of State, a tough, plain-spoken dark-haired woman named Elizabeth Halderman. A former U.S. Ambassador to the United Nations, Halderman was a gifted diplomat who famously didn't take any shit from anyone. She was one of the few politicians Christine Cobalt actually liked.

At the Fury's side was a short, rat-faced, slightly hunch-backed man by the name of Anatoly Argentov.

Argentov was introduced to the heaving mass of

journalists as a senior official from the Russian Foreign Ministry but Cobalt knew from her briefing that he was actually a senior agent in the K.G.B., one of Russia's best and most experienced spies, and their primary expert on *her*.

She also knew a couple of other interesting things about her opponents: like how the Fury hated speaking to women as equals. That had been another reason for bringing Halderman.

She was also aware that he despised being called *Sergeant* Furin, his old rank before he had acquired his abilities. On becoming all-powerful in Russia, he'd been promoted directly from sergeant all the way to the highest rank, Marshal.

'Thank you, everyone! Thank you!' Cobalt said into her microphone. 'Please excuse us now. Sergeant Furin and I have some things to discuss.'

The journalists shouted more questions as they were ushered out of the hall.

For the next thirty minutes, sitting across a table from each other in the glittering ballroom, they hashed out various matters that were of importance to their respective nations.

Cobalt and her Secretary of State for America. The Fury and Agent Argentov for Russia.

Argentov was speaking. The Fury fiddled with one of his red gloves, looking profoundly bored.

'—if your President keeps saying such lies about our country,' Argentov said, 'the Fury will come over there and crush his larynx.'

'No. He won't, Mr Argentov,' Cobalt said. 'Because I'd be there and Sergeant Furin and I have the exact same powers. Do I have to keep saying this?'

'Our country would just like some respect from the White House, that is all—'

'Respect?' Cobalt's eyes flashed. 'Perhaps you're forgetting the *assassination* of our former Secretary of Defence on the *Caribbean Star*. That plan was intended not only to kill him but also to sink the ship and drown six thousand passengers to cover it up.'

'Now, wait just a—' Argentov stammered.

'Or the time two of his boys tried to *kill my husband and daughter*!' Cobalt said.

'They did that on their own, the foolish boys,' Argentov said quickly. 'They were not authorised—'

The U.S. Secretary of State jumped in, nodding at the Fury. '*He* has to control his sons because your government can't!'

'They were young, rash . . .' Argentov said.

'They tried to kill my family,' Christine Cobalt said flatly.

'So you killed them.'

'I sure did.'

The Secretary of State said, 'Which means you've now only got three of his supersons left, plus the smart one you've got hidden away. While we've got all of ours—'

'*You won't always be here.*'

It was said softly, in a whisper.

By the Fury.

It was the first time he'd spoken since they had retreated to this private space and the way he said it was chilling.

'Excuse me?' Cobalt said.

'I said, you won't always be here, Dr Cobalt. Our powers are the same, but I am younger. You will die first eventually. And we both know your children are no match for me.'

Secretary of State Halderman kicked back her chair and stood up. 'Okay. I think it's time for a recess—'

'I wish to speak with Dr Cobalt alone,' the Fury said. 'Hero to hero.'

Cobalt glanced at Liz Halderman. They had anticipated that he might ask for a private chat with her, but they weren't sure what it might be about.

She nodded. 'Okay.'

The Secretary of State and Argentov left. Now, it was only Christine Cobalt and the Fury in the grand room.

'What?' Cobalt asked.

'I have a proposition.'

'Okay . . .?'

'We mate,' the Fury said.

Christine Cobalt blinked. 'I don't think so.'

The Fury said, 'Your offspring have only half your powers. So do mine. Because their other parents were regular humans. But if *we* produced a child . . .'

Christine Cobalt was speechless with shock.

'We could create a dynasty of powered individuals to rule the world,' the Fury said. 'You and I. We dispense with politicians, parliaments. *And we impose order.* No wars. No corruption.'

'No way,' Cobalt said.

'Why not?'

'I'm married.'

'The future of the species outweighs such a relationship. Why really?'

'Because: you.'

'What about me?' The Fury looked genuinely confused.

'You're repulsive and a psychopath.'

'*Bitch.* Always thought you were so smart, even up in the ice. With your education and your science.'

'Smarter than you. And just as strong.'

'After you die, I will kill all your children, one by one, and your bookish little husband, too.'

'Go fuck yourself.'

'And I will tear down your country and I will make your people *feel* it. I will kidnap your President and, live on television, rape his wife in front of him.'

'Really, go fuck yourself,' Cobalt said.

'Mate with me.'

Christine Cobalt stood and headed to the door.

'This conversation is over.'

'You could be immortal!' the Fury called after her. 'Our children would be gods!'

Opening the door for the Secretary of State and Argentov, Cobalt said, 'Mortal's fine by me if that's the price.'

The Secretary of State and Argentov re-entered, both looking perplexed.

Walking back to the table beside Cobalt, the Secretary whispered, 'Everything all right?'

'Tell you later.'

As they all sat back down at the negotiating table, the Fury said, 'You have three daughters, Cobalt. After you are gone, I will make them my concubines. Or perhaps just your natural daughter.'

Christine Cobalt could only stare at him.

When she got home, she recounted that exchange to Cassie.

Having just turned twenty-one, Cassie had already decided to go into Witness Protection.

After her mother returned from the Paris summit and told her of that conversation with the Fury, Cassie sped up the process.

◼ WITSEC ◼

U.S. MARSHALS WESTERN DIVISION FIELD OFFICE DENVER, COLORADO NINE YEARS AGO

The woman who sat across from Cassie smelled of cigarettes, wasn't in shape, and wore a cheap rumpled suit. A pair of reading glasses seemed permanently perched on her nose.

Cassie loved her instantly.

U.S. Marshal Connie-Anne Walters was one of those law enforcement types who just radiated competence.

It was in the way she spoke—gruff and curt—and the way she carried herself. She was in her fifties and it looked like literally nothing rattled her.

But beneath her gruff voice was a kind nature, which was probably why, Cassie figured, Connie-Anne Walters had gone into the witness protection business.

Sitting beside Cassie that day, gripping her hand

supportively, was Golden Gary. He wore a subdued outfit for the occasion, plain civilian clothes and a trucker cap. That was a big concession for Gary.

Connie-Anne Walters said, 'You'll have to cut all ties with friends: schoolfriends, boyfriends, friends with benefits. No social media, Facebook, Instagram, and no Tinder—God, especially no Tinder. Fucking Tinder, it's the bane of my existence.'

'Heavens, why?' Golden Gary said. He loved Tinder. Well, Grindr.

'Lost a mob guy because he couldn't stay off that damn app,' Connie-Anne said. 'Girl he swiped right on turned out to be a paid killer.'

'I'm gonna have to be more careful,' Gary said thoughtfully.

'Do you really need to be here?' Connie-Anne glowered at him.

'He's here for moral support,' Cassie said.

'And *fashion* support,' Gary added. 'Not that you need any, Marshal Tough Lady. You got the whole deadpan rough-edged hard-bitten cop thing *down*.'

Connie-Anne kept going. 'Avoid public places. If you have to go to the mall, go at quiet times. If you have to travel, go by car. Airports are dangerous. Although, can you fly?'

Cassie gave a noncommittal shrug.

'Wouldn't need an airport if you could, I guess. I never WITSEC'd the kid of a superhero before.'

'What about my name?' Cassie asked.

'We find it's best that people use their real first name. You look up when someone calls it. You'll get a new surname, though.'

'Job?'

'Given who your mom is and your education, we were able to pull some strings. J.P.L. in L.A. Great security and almost everyone has top-secret clearance, so they don't ask questions.'

'I love it.'

'You'll start out doing the night shift. Keep you out of sight for a while.'

'Fine.'

Connie-Anne shifted in her chair. Behind her, out the window, Cassie could see the Rockies.

'Kid. Listen. Witness Protection isn't easy. You gotta be alert every single day. One slip-up is all it takes and you're dead. Watch for tails. Cars lurking about. Be suspicious of anyone wanting to buy you a drink, male or female—'

'Or gender fluid and non-binary,' Gary added.

Connie-Anne ignored him. 'And one more thing.'

'Yes?'

'Don't fall in love. Love makes people drop their guard and do stupid things and that just gives me a headache.'

'Okay.' Cassie smiled.

'Beyond that,' Connie-Anne said, 'I'm your point person. I will be the *only* United States Marshal who ever calls you or calls on you. I will not text you. I will not email you. And I will not delegate this. If someone says they're calling on my behalf, if they say they're my boss, if they say I'm dying in the hospital and I want my last words to be with you, *they are lying*. Got that?'

'Yes, ma'am,' Cassie said.

'Yes, ma'am!' Gary echoed. He nudged Cassie with his elbow. 'Geez, she's good. Although I don't think she can physically smile.'

'Ma'am. Name's Connie-Anne, kid.' She gave Gary a deadpan smile. 'And you, I like you. You're kinda funny.'

Shortly after, they stepped into a cubicle outside Connie-Anne's office.

A geeky-looking computer guy named Emmett Tibbet sat waiting for them with his fingers poised above the keys of a computer.

Connie-Anne said, 'Emmett here will handle all your new IDs. Passport, California driver's licence.'

Emmett stared at Cassie, starstruck. 'Are you really her daughter?' he asked.

'Yep.'

'*Whoa.*'

Connie-Anne groaned. 'Yo. Emmett. Stop fanboying and build the fake IDs, all right.'

'Right. Copy. Roger that,' Emmett said, turning back to his computer.

Connie-Anne gave Cassie a look over her nose-mounted reading glasses. 'Kid, did I say no Tinder?'

LOS ANGELES
TODAY

Cassie's phone rang, loud and sudden. She was still in her kitchen with Trey.

The caller ID read: CONNIE-ANNE.

Cassie answered it. 'Thought you might call.'

'You okay?'

It was hard to put it into words. The brutal and rapid elimination of her noble half-siblings. It was too much, too violent, and happening way too fast.

'Not really,' was all Cassie could say. 'Kind of on the ragged edge here.'

Connie-Anne said, 'I can't imagine. But you're safe?'

'For now.'

'You can talk, this line is secure and nobody but me

knows where you are.'

'Connie-Anne, should I come out? Face him?'

'Can you beat him?'

'No.'

Connie-Anne sighed over the phone line. Cassie could almost picture her in her reading glasses, pinching the bridge of her nose.

'Aw, kid, I don't know how you can think clearly at a time like this. Your mom just died and now he's here, moving across the country killing the other Cobalts one by one.'

'I don't know what to do.'

'Then maybe this'll help,' Connie-Anne said. 'The C.I.A. just called WITSEC, said they had someone who wanted to talk to you. My boss checked it out—it's legit—so he asked me to pass it on. A Russian spy we got in custody wants to speak with you. Name's Anatoly Argentov. Know him?'

'He was at the Paris summit with the Fury and my mom.'

'Well, he got busted here a year ago running a spy ring outta the Russian consulate in L.A. and now, today, he says he can help you. Normally, I'd throw this in the bullshit file, but . . .'

'Where is he?' Cassie asked.

'L.A. Federal Building.'

'What have I got to lose?'

'Then listen up. A C.I.A. spook named Shawna Eason will meet you in the underground lot and let you in via a secure elevator so no-one will—'

'I don't think my anonymity matters anymore, Connie-Anne. Set it up.'

'All right, will do. Hey, kid. Good luck.'

'Thanks, Connie-Anne. Thanks for everything.'

Cassie hung up.

U.S. MARSHALS WESTERN DIVISION FIELD OFFICE DENVER, COLORADO TODAY

In her office in Denver, Connie-Anne hung up her phone. She was reaching for her file on Cassie when—

—a sonic boom rang out from outside.

Connie-Anne looked up, her face setting itself in a tight grimace.

'Shit,' she whispered to no-one.

A moment later, she heard the sound of smashing glass in a nearby office: a window breaking.

He was here.

Then screams.

Then gunshots.

U.S. Marshals didn't like Russian superheroes bursting into their offices. But their bullets were useless against him.

The door to Connie-Anne's office was kicked in.

And the Fury of Russia stood before her, gigantic in his full red superhero suit, glaring down at Connie-Anne Walters through his fearsome facemask.

'United States Marshal Constance-Anne Walters?' he said.

Connie said nothing.

'Of the Federal Witness Protection Program, western division? Case officer for the natural daughter of the late hero, Cobalt?'

Connie-Anne eyed him coolly.

Then, with total calmness, she pulled out a cigarette, lit it and took a long drag.

'Who's askin'?' she said.

The Fury cocked his head.

'You think you're funny?' he said. 'I can make this very painful for you.'

'Do your worst, motherfucker,' Connie-Anne said.

The Fury stepped inside her office and slammed the door shut behind him.

FEDERAL BUILDING, LOS ANGELES
TODAY

When Cassie arrived at the Federal Building near LAX twenty minutes later, a C.I.A. agent named Shawna Eason was waiting for her in the underground garage.

Eason whisked Cassie through every security check-point without even stopping and up to the holding floor with its interrogation rooms.

While his features hadn't changed, Anatoly Argentov had aged considerably since the Paris summit. His hair had receded but he still had his long rat nose and cunning eyes.

The K.G.B. spy wore an orange prison jumpsuit, ankle cuffs and handcuffs. These were linked through ringbolts on a table which itself was screwed to the floor.

Cassie sat opposite him.

It was just the two of them in the bland cinderblock room, but Cassie knew there were people watching through the two-way mirror.

She didn't care.

Argentov grinned, revealing sickly yellow teeth. 'The fabled natural daughter of Cobalt. The one who hid.'

'You said you could help me,' Cassie said simply.

Argentov nodded. 'It was wise to hide. The others, your half-siblings, living so publicly, he knew all about them long ago. The Army poster boy. The policeman in Chicago. The troubled genius. The funny gay one. But not you. You are a mystery. We don't even know what powers you have.'

'Get to the point.'

'He hated your mother. Hated her with a passion. Fate threw them together in the Arctic. In no other circumstances would they have ever met. She was everything he was not. American. Educated. Articulate. Poised. And she had money.'

'Not a lot. She was a scientist.'

'He grew up in poverty. Not American poverty, *Russian* poverty. Bitter cold, starvation. He barely had an eighth-grade education. Then the Russian Army, even more bitter. His name is no idle propaganda. He is anger. He is rage. He is fury.'

'You got ten seconds to say what this has to do with me?'

'After they were infected, he felt a kinship with your mother. Two people with identical powers, alone in the world. He propositioned her at the summit and she rebuffed him.'

'I know. She told me,' Cassie said.

'It made him hate her even more.'

'He asked her to mate with him. At least my dad bought her dinner first—'

'That she was married to a studious little man only enraged him more. He is literally the most powerful man on Earth and she chooses a bespectacled nerd over him.'

'My father was a wonderful man. My mother loved him till the day he died.'

'You know, in Russia, we also have a clever one.'

'What?'

'Like your Cobalt Black. A Russian child who got a superbrain.'

'So?' Cassie said.

'Our genius analysed the Fury. His mind. His motivations . . .' Argentov leaned forward, again showing his ugly yellow canines. *The Fury now considers you to be her.*'

'Why?'

'Because you are natural-born. The others came from test tubes, from the seeds of men selected by your government for their strength, their fighting skills or their IQs. Seeds that were inserted into eggs donated by your mother. But not you.'

'Go on.'

'The Fury *wants* you. Like he wanted her. His pathology runs deep, born from the miserable life he lived until the day he acquired his powers. The poor Russian sergeant wants to own the brilliant American woman. Your half-siblings, he will kill them without a moment's thought. But you face a fate far worse. He wants to make you his bride, his sex slave, his leashed pet in front of the world. My point is: since he could not do this with your mother, *he wants to do it with you.*'

Cassie leaned back, horrified.

'Why are you telling me this?' she said.

At that, Argentov threw his head back and cackled crazily.

'Little girl. I just wanted to see the look on your face when you found out.'

His cackling grew in intensity . . . and mania. Cassie got up and left the room.

The sound of his laughter followed her down the corridor.

Trey was waiting for her in a cubicle farm at the end of the hallway. 'Well?' he asked.

'You don't want to know,' Cassie said.

'I'm your husband.'

'That's why you don't want to know.'

The C.I.A. lady, Eason, came up to them. 'The Fury just attacked Witness Protection headquarters in Denver. Grabbed Walters. She didn't talk so he killed her.'

Cassie gasped. 'Connie-Anne? Holy shit.'

'But then he found a computer guy, Emmett something. Tortured the poor kid till he pulled up your file. The Fury knows everything about you, what you look like, where you work, who you married, and your home address here in L.A.'

'Jesus,' Trey said.

'He knows where we live . . .' Cassie said. She began to hyperventilate. And he'd murdered Connie-Anne. Gruff yet kind, the U.S. Marshal had stayed loyal to Cassie to the end, till he killed her.

'Cassie, you okay—?' Trey said.

Cassie was breathing faster and faster. 'I can't—I need—I've got to go somewhere I can—'

She was losing it.

Trey took her firmly by the arm and looked her squarely in the eye.

'Hey,' he said. 'I got you.'

Cassie blinked uncomprehendingly.

Trey added, 'I may not have any superpowers, but I got your back. Come with me.'

He said it with such calm assurance, she settled down

a bit. He guided her gently down the hallway toward the elevators.

As they walked, Cassie regathered herself and threw a sideways look at her young husband.

'You do have a superpower, by the way,' she said.

'What's that?'

'Bravery.'

'Yeah? When was I brave?' Trey asked.

'When you met my mother the first time,' Cassie said.

◼◼◼◼◼◼ TREY ◼◼◼◼

DILLON, MONTANA
FOUR YEARS AGO

Every couple has to do it and every couple dreads it: meeting the parents.

What few couples have to negotiate, however, is the situation where one of the parents is a living national treasure and possesses superpowers.

Thus it was that Cassie and Trey came to the small town of Dillon, Montana, the site of her parents' new ranch house, with its many miles of empty surrounding land.

In addition to his glasses, Trey was wearing his Sunday best: a sports coat, shirt and tie.

As they entered the ranch house, Cassie's dad was waiting for them, in his wheelchair. Cobalt was nowhere to be seen.

'So this is him, huh?' Arnold Cobalt said, rolling over and extending his hand. 'Arnold Cobalt.'

'Trey Cassowitz, sir.'

'Please, call me Arnie. Usually boyfriends are afraid of meeting a girl's father, but I'm under no illusions here. It's Mom who's the scary one. Wanna beer?'

'No, thank you.'

'Mind if I have one?'

'Not at all.'

Arnie turned to Cassie. 'I like him already! Sit, sit. Yeah, I imagine it's hard to "meet the parents" when one of them can literally break you in half. Cassie's mom is out back in the study. Just got a call from the Joint Chiefs about something or other.'

Cassie and Trey sat on the couch facing her dad.

'Okay . . .' Trey said.

Arnie added, 'Did I mention she could break you in half?'

'Dad!' Cassie said.

Arnie Cobalt laughed. He was loving this. 'Cassie says you're an engineer at SpaceX.'

'I am,' Trey said. 'In rocket propellant. Cassie and I met during a J.P.L.–SpaceX collaboration. I'd see this mysterious female engineer finishing the night shift. Took me a month to work up the courage to ask her on a date—'

At that moment, Christine Cobalt entered the living room in her full white-and-sky-blue superhero uniform.

She had always been tall, but the uniform made her seem taller, made her dominate a room, any room.

Gentleman that he was, Trey stood up instantly.

'So this is him?' the great hero said, her voice booming. 'Trey, right? Trey Cassowitz.'

'Yes, ma'am.'

'Please, call me Chris.'

'Sure . . . Chris.'

Cobalt stepped around and behind her husband's wheelchair. 'Trey. Cassie here is my only natural child—'

She cut herself off, turned to Arnie.

'Did you tell him about how I could break him in half?'

'Of course,' Arnie said gleefully.

'Well, there's not much I can add,' Christine Cobalt said. 'Break her heart and I break you, Trey.'

Cassie squirmed like every girl in history who had brought a guy home to meet her parents.

But Trey wasn't squirming. His eyes stayed level. He was still standing.

'Ma'am,' he said. 'I thought your daughter was super

long before she told me she was *your* daughter. I love her, so it's infinitely more likely she'll break my heart first.'

Cassie assessed the looks on her parents' faces.

Her dad was a sweetheart. She knew he'd like Trey.

But her mom was a different story. Years of being a superhero and mingling with presidents, politicians and generals had made her jaded, untrusting.

But this answer from Trey, delivered so calmly, had landed.

Christine and Arnie Cobalt exchanged looks, then they both burst out laughing.

'Good answer, Trey Cassowitz,' the great Cobalt said. 'Sit down, son. I like the cut of your jib.'

FEDERAL BUILDING, LOS ANGELES
TODAY

Cassie and Trey stepped out of the elevator and into the Federal Building's underground parking lot.

Like the rest of America, today it was empty. People had stayed home to huddle with their families as their country was attacked.

Cassie slid into their car and slammed the door, breathing deeply, trying to calm down. Trey dropped into the driver's seat beside her.

'How're you feeling?' he asked.

'Little better, thanks,' Cassie said.

He keyed the ignition and the radio came on.

The newsreader was saying, '—*Air Force Two was spotted landing at LAX ten minutes ago. But the White House has not issued any statements as to what the Vice President might be doing in Los Angeles.*'

'The Vice President is in L.A.,' Cassie said. 'That's weird.'

Trey scowled. 'The guy is weird, one of those evangelical politicians. Always talking about prayer and God and then he goes and cuts some program like food stamps.'

Cassie nodded. 'My mom agreed with you. She hated him. Had a run-in with him that she never forgot. I saw it go down because it happened when he accompanied her on a congressional visit to my lab.'

◼◼◼◼◼◼◼ THE VICE PRESIDENT ◼◼◼◼◼◼◼

J.P.L. FACILITY, DOWNTOWN L.A.
THREE YEARS AGO

Cassie watched them walk through her workplace, guided by her famous mother and the director of the Jet Propulsion Laboratory.

Of course, none of the congressional delegates—two senators and the Vice President of the United States: the men in charge of NASA's budget—or any of their retinues knew who Cassie was or that she worked here. All they knew was that the great Cobalt had a special place in her heart for J.P.L. and liked to make sure it received ongoing funding.

As the tour took place, Cassie hid in plain sight,

wearing the full-body white cleansuit that all the J.P.L. satellite builders wore. She literally faded into the background.

The director guided the congressional party into the high-pressure test chamber, with its reinforced walls and heavy iron door.

Cassie watched them from the adjoining control room, through six-inch-thick Lexan glass. She heard the director's voice through a pair of headphones.

'. . . and this is where we test our gas-giant observation satellites,' he was saying.

The two senators and the Vice President nodded knowingly, even though Cassie was pretty sure they didn't know what that even meant.

They looked around the chamber with its sturdy walls and big iron door.

Yellow-and-black warning signs blared: DANGER: PRESSURISED ENVIRONMENT!

On the door was a lever marked EMERGENCY RELEASE. In the middle of the chamber sat a very cool-looking silver satellite. It was a sphere the size of a refrigerator and it was Cassie's project.

The director went over to it. 'This observation satellite is destined for Jupiter. We're going to fly her right into its atmosphere and collect every sample we can.'

'Fly her to Jupiter.' The Vice President nodded sagely.

'Goodness me, the brilliance behind this science is just a miracle from God.'

The director coughed, uncertain how to respond.

Out of desperation, he indicated one of the warning signs around them: DECOMPRESSION RULES IN EFFECT. OBSERVE SAFE EXIT PROTOCOLS.

'To make sure the satellite can handle the extreme conditions of the Jovian atmosphere, we have to test her in all kinds of wild environments. You saw the Cold Space Lab next door. It can bring the temperature down to almost zero Kelvin. This is the high-pressure test chamber. It can mimic the extreme *pressure* of Jupiter's atmosphere. We can crank it up to one thousand atmospheres.'

'Meaning?' the Vice President asked.

'Meaning, Mr Vice President, if someone shuts that door, don't inhale.'

'Why not?'

The director said, 'Your lungs hold approximately six litres of air. Inhale that air at five atmospheres and the air expands five times to thirty litres. If pressure is lost, that expanded air will explode your lungs and blow out your whole chest.'

'Dear Lord.' In addition to being a Christian, the Vice President was a known germaphobe.

He nodded at a complex-looking laser nearby.

'And what is that?'

'That,' the director said, 'is a Morton-Simpson cutting laser.'

'How much is it costing us?' one of the senators asked with a laugh.

'A lot,' Christine Cobalt said. 'But since it can slice through raw titanium and thus build these amazing satellites, it's worth it.'

The group left the chamber, but as they did, the Vice President touched Christine Cobalt on the shoulder.

'Dr Cobalt, a word.'

Christine Cobalt remained behind in the high-pressure chamber with the Vice President.

At the same time, Cassie's companions in the control room also left. Moving last of all, Cassie saw her mother and the Vice President stay in the pressure chamber, so she lingered behind in the control room, unseen by either of them, and listened to their private conversation through her headset.

'You need to pick a side in the coming election, Doctor,' the Vice President said.

'With respect, Mr Vice President, I don't endorse one side or another. I serve whichever party is in office.'

'The President would like—and quite frankly, expects—your support over the coming months.'

Christine Cobalt said, 'Whoever is President after the

election will have my support, sir.'

The Vice President looked around them. 'We know the causes you like, Doctor. Like this place, NASA, the ASPCA. We can always cut their funding, you know.'

Christine Cobalt's eyes went hard. 'Are you threatening me?'

Cassie watched in astonishment from the control room.

The Vice President gave her mother an oily smile. 'I just want to make sure you're on the right side. God bless you.'

And with those words, he sidled out.

Cassie shook her head as she remembered that day.

'It took all my mom's restraint not to punch out the Vice President of the United States. Unfortunately, the jerk got re-elected.'

She blinked the thought away, tried to refocus.

Trey had his cell phone out. On its screen was a news website showing a map of the Fury's progress so far.

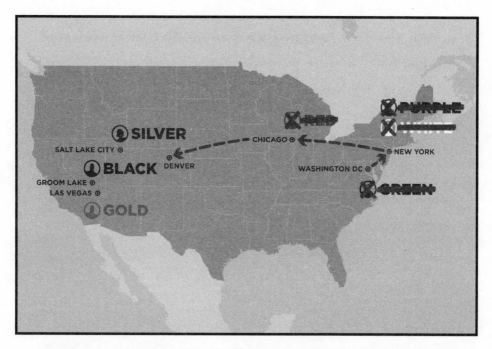

Cassie examined it. 'Okay. The Fury's still moving west. He just hit Denver, which means Silvy will be next in Salt Lake City.'

Trey frowned. 'You think the Fury would hit her? She chose not to be a hero.'

'He'll hit her. While any of us are alive, we're a threat.'

'I've never met Cobalt Silver but your dad liked her a lot, even though she wasn't his kid.'

'My dad acted as a surrogate father to all the Cobalt kids when they were young—well, all of them except Black. Dad didn't care that they weren't technically his. He helped Silvia work through some heavy stuff—'

Cassie's cell phone rang.

The screen read: NO CALLER ID.

She and Trey swapped worried looks. Cassie answered it. 'Hello?'

'Cassie. It's Silvia,' a woman's voice said. 'How you doing?'

Cassie exhaled. 'Awful. You?'

'It's like watching the Grim Reaper walking down your street, stopping at every house, and waiting for him to arrive at your door,' said her half-sister Silvia, otherwise known as Cobalt Silver.

THE CATHEDRAL OF THE MADELEINE
SALT LAKE CITY, UTAH
TWO YEARS AGO

Cassie walked with Silvia and Golden Gary in a garden behind the grand Catholic cathedral in Salt Lake City. It was a beautiful and serene place. Over the high walls, you could see the mountains.

Cassie eyed the walls. They were the reason Silvia lived here.

Cassie wore blue jeans, a t-shirt and Nike running shoes.

Golden Gary wore a designer denim jacket with gold piping and matching jeans plus glittery gold brogues.

Silvia wore the grey habit of a novice nun.

Gary nodded at it. 'I gotta say, I love the look, Silvy. I think I wore the same outfit to a saints-and-sinners party at Planet Hollywood last year. Only it had a slit up the leg and I wore nine-inch red pumps.'

'Gary!' Cassie exclaimed.

Silvia just smiled. 'It's okay. I love our Gary. I pray for him.'

'Even when I'm living in Vegas, kissing boys, and generally misbehaving?' Gary asked.

'Especially then.'

'Wait,' Gary said, 'do you really pray for me?'

'Every night, Gary. And for you, too, Cassie.'

Cassie got serious. 'Why this?'

Silvia looked out at the mountains with a faraway stare. 'I've thought about it a lot. These powers we have, they're not of this Earth.'

'That's no reason to stop having sex, girl,' Gary said.

'People call us gods,' Silvia went on. 'But I don't think it's healthy to be a god. Cobalt Black, of course, disagrees with me.'

'He's such a douche,' Gary said.

'What will you do here?' Cassie asked.

'They're letting me run the women's shelter. It's inside the cathedral grounds, so the media can't get to me. And it gives the women who come here comfort to know that Cobalt Silver is sleeping under the same roof as them. Their abusive husbands and boyfriends aren't going to get past me.'

'Nice,' Cassie said.

'Yeah,' Gary agreed.

'I mean, it's not national or showy, but it's still helping—'

'It's perfect.'

'Agree again.'

Silvia nodded. 'Thanks, I appreciate you guys supporting my decision. Not everyone has.'

'Are you kidding?' Cassie said. 'This is absolutely right for you.'

Gary nodded. 'Fucking-A. Oh, shit, can I say fuck in here? God, now I just said shit. Oh, whatever. We love you, Silvy Bear, and we support your decision even if it means you'll *never have sex again*.'

Silver and Cassie laughed at that.

'Just sayin',' Gary said.

It was a rare moment of joy.

Silvia was still on the phone.

'I know religion isn't all that popular these days, Cassie, but will you do me a favour and pray for me?'

'I will,' Cassie said.

'Cassie?'

'Yes, Silvia.'

'I'm going to die, little sister, and I don't want to die. I want to live. But hate is coming for me. And after I'm dead, he'll come for you, too. And by the way, Cobalt

Black isn't the smartest of us all. He has pure intelligence, sure, but you have two things Black doesn't.'

'What are they?'

'Imagination and the humility to listen to other people's ideas. If anyone can figure the Fury out, it's you. Please figure him out and beat him. For those of us who couldn't. I have to go now.'

The line went dead.

SALT LAKE CITY, UTAH
TODAY

A red streak shot across the pale-blue sky above Salt Lake City.

The streets were largely empty, but screams could be heard.

'That's him!'

'He's here!'

Silvia—Cobalt Silver—stood alone outside the magnificent front entrance to the cathedral.

The Fury of Russia landed on the open plaza in front of her.

He started striding forward.

He stood a full foot taller than Silvia. Compared to her soft and formless grey nun's habit, everything about him seemed bigger, more menacing.

His carbon-ceramic mask seemed sharper. His helmet, armour and gauntlets seemed more hard-edged.

'I will not fight you,' Silvia said.

'You still must die.' Through the mask, his voice even seemed more inhuman.

Silvia stood her ground.

'I can smell your fear,' he said.

'You won't win,' she replied.

'Who will stop me if you will not fight me? Your god?'

'Maybe.'

The Fury said, 'There is no god but me. If God chooses who lives and who dies, then I am God now. No-one can stop me exercising my will.'

'There's only one God and you aren't Him,' Silvia said.

The Fury tilted his head as he took another step forward. 'Is that so? If we allow that your God does actually exist, *then He is permitting all this to happen*. He is permitting me to do all this. All this killing. All this wanton destruction—'

'I know someone who can beat you,' Cobalt Silver said firmly.

That actually made the Fury stop.

He was a few feet in front of her now. He towered over her.

'The one in Las Vegas?' he asked. 'The one who wears gold?'

'He's good, but no, it's not him.'

'No person on this Earth can beat me,' the Fury said. 'I will kill you all and I will rule the cosseted, pampered people of this land with an iron fist. I will crush their spirit with unspeakable violence.'

He was inches away from her now. Silvia just stared up at him . . .

. . . and closed her eyes. Despite herself, she was quivering.

She started praying, 'Hail Mary, full of grace . . .' as the Fury clasped his hands on either side of her head and started squeezing.

FEDERAL BUILDING, LOS ANGELES
TODAY

Someone was pounding on the window of Cassie's car in the garage of the Federal Building. A United States Marine.

He was holding out a cell phone.

'Ma'am? Miss? I got a call for you! The Chairman of the Joint Chiefs of Staff.'

Cassie lowered the window and took the phone. She put it on speaker so Trey could hear.

'Hello?' she said.

'Ms Cassowitz,' a deep voice said from the other end of the line. 'This is General Hank Stevenson. Cobalt Silver has just been taken out in Utah and now things have got worse.'

'Worse?' Cassie said.

He'd killed Silvy. Sweet, gentle Silvy. It was hard to imagine how things could get any worse.

The general said, 'We were wondering what the Fury's remaining sons were doing while he was here. Well, now we know what two of the three were doing: the Furies of Leningrad and Stalingrad just took out our entire naval base at Pearl Harbor. Came from the other side. Now they're heading for Los Angeles.'

As they heard this, Trey Googled the news on his phone.

The cable news websites were all over it: photos and footage of the smoking ruins of Honolulu; half-sunk destroyers and carriers; plus a digital map showing two red dots moving across the Pacific Ocean, heading toward L.A.

Text at the bottom of the screen read: TWO OF FURY'S SONS LEVEL HONOLULU.

The general said, 'With only three of you left—Cobalt Gold in Las Vegas, Cobalt Black at Groom Lake and you in L.A.—he's bringing in his boys to finish the job and start their takeover of our country.'

'Is there anything you can do to help us?' Cassie asked.

'We can't stop this guy when he's alone. With his sons at his side, he's unbeatable.'

Cassie said, 'Did the President say anything? He used to talk with my mother.'

There was an awkward silence over the phone line.

Then the general said, 'The President has instructed all U.S. forces to stand down.'

'*What?!*'

'The President is hoping when the Fury is done, he might be able to negotiate some kind of settlement with him.'

'When the Fury's *done*? You mean when he's killed all of us.'

'I'm sorry.'

'You can't negotiate with this man, you must know that.'

'My orders come from the President himself.'

'So you're leaving us to die,' Cassie said. 'We're inconvenient now.'

'There's literally nothing we can do. I really am sorry.'

Cassie bit her lip in thought. 'How long till his two sons in Hawaii get to L.A.?'

'At their current speed, three hours.'

'Do you know the whereabouts of the oldest one, the Fury of Moscow? And the smart one, Sevastopol?'

'No and no.'

'All right, then, thanks,' Cassie said. 'I have to go and die now.'

She hung up before he could say anything more.

Cassie looked at her husband.

'Still glad you married me?' she asked.

In response, Trey gave her the finger: the one with his wedding ring on it.

'Till death do us part, baby,' he said.

'No military, no support.'

'I'm with you till the end, pathetic regular human male that I am.'

'You know, that's what my dad liked most about you,' Cassie said.

▬▬▬▬▬▬▬ DAD ▬▬▬▬▬▬▬

SPACEX FACILITY, LONG BEACH
FOUR YEARS AGO

Given her dad's love of knowledge, for his birthday four years ago—shortly after he had met Trey—Cassie and Trey arranged to take him on an after-hours private tour of Trey's workplace at SpaceX.

Of course, Arnold Cobalt—being pushed around in his wheelchair—adored it.

'This place is *amazing*!' he exclaimed as Cassie wheeled him past a wide round tank filled with goopy white super-cooled liquid nitrogen.

Trey said, 'That's the nitrogen fuel mix. It's semiliquid now but it'll be in a solid state for launch.'

As they stepped into the next lab, Cassie said, 'This one is my favourite.'

In this next room was a long, straight, waist-high track of some sort.

'What. Is. That?' Dad said.

Trey smiled. 'Our electromagnetic rail gun. For orbital launches. To get Elon to Mars.'

'A rail gun.' Dad shook his head. 'You two are so lucky to work in this era of science—'

He coughed suddenly, explosively. 'You okay, Dad?' Cassie asked.

'It's nothing. Had it since the last surgery. That punch did more than break my spine. We non-superheroes have to deal with simple human frailty, you know.'

Later that night, their excursion over, Cassie pushed her dad into her modest little house. Trey had gone back to his place.

'I like him,' her father said. 'He's decent.'

'They say girls marry men who are like their fathers,' Cassie said.

'Then he's also uncommonly smart and handsome. Think you'll marry him?'

'Yes,' Cassie said firmly.

'Is he aware of this?'

'I think he plans to ask soon.'

Her dad nodded. 'I like plans. Always have a plan. Whether you're doing a road trip or mapping out the rest of your life, it's always good to have a plan.'

'Yes, grasshopper.' Cassie smiled. She'd heard this before.

She started making tea in the adjoining kitchen.

'We didn't have a plan that night, when those two Russian boys came,' Dad said. 'Now we do. That's why your mother bought the ranch house in Montana and all the land around it, so we'll see anyone coming.'

Cassie frowned at him. 'Come on, Dad. We couldn't have anticipated—'

'It was a mistake.'

'You couldn't have known those two boys would do something as crazy as that.'

'That was exactly my mistake. No-one anticipates "crazy", yet crazy can win against the odds.'

'I don't understand.' Cassie handed him his tea.

'Let me tell you a story,' her dad said. 'Your mother's father was a cranky old dude, but smart. He was unbeatable at cards—bridge, 500—because he could count every card. After three hands he could tell you every card still in your hand. Nobody could beat him. Till I came along.'

'How'd you do it?' Cassie said.

'Unpredictable calls. Wild plays. I didn't play for the

cards I had. I played for a few good breaks. I played crazy and I beat him.'

'How'd he take it?'

'He refused to play with me anymore,' Dad said.

'Sore loser,' Cassie said.

Her dad nodded. 'As only someone used to winning can be. That was also how I beat him: the guy who's used to winning always thinks he'll win.'

He looked up sharply, changing the topic completely.

'Oh, and I liked the way your man handled your mother at the ranch!'

'I know!' Cassie said. 'Me, too!'

Cassie and Trey's little Jeep pulled out of the underground garage of the Federal Building near Los Angeles International Airport and zoomed up the on-ramp to the 405.

The usually congested freeway opened wide before them, bare and deserted, as most of the city's population remained in their homes fearfully watching the day's events on TV.

Cassie and Trey had barely driven onto the freeway when something very strange happened.

Six L.A.P.D. cop cars swept out from the on-ramp behind them, their sirens blaring, lights flashing.

Trey pulled over onto the shoulder, slowing down to allow the black-and-whites to go past and get to whatever emergency they were racing to.

Only the squad cars didn't go past.

They surrounded the Jeep.

A cop in the lead car waved for Trey to come to a stop while he called over the loudspeaker: '*Mr Cassowitz! Ms Cassowitz! Please pull over!*'

'What should we do?' Trey asked.

'Stop,' Cassie said.

It was only when they came to a complete stop that Cassie saw the Suburbans.

There were three of them—three big black Chevy Suburbans with blacked-out windows—lurking just behind the cop cars.

One of the black Suburbans drove right past all the police cars and pulled up next to Cassie and Trey's Jeep. Two men in suits and sunglasses leapt out of it with pistols drawn while a third man opened the Suburban's rear door.

Out of that door stepped the Vice President of the United States.

'Ms Cassowitz,' he said. 'I'm here to help. If you want to survive this day, I need you and your husband to come with me right now.'

LOS ANGELES INTERNATIONAL AIRPORT
TODAY

The motorcade of cop cars and Secret Service Suburbans sped toward LAX.

Cassie and Trey sat awkwardly in the back of the middle Suburban, beside the Vice President himself.

'Dear Lord, what a day,' the Vice President said. 'A terrible, terrible day. We need to get you to the airport and out of this city, young lady. Make you safe.'

The motorcade swept around the perimeter fence of the airport and then rushed without stopping through a guarded gate before suddenly every car in the convoy pulled over and stopped while the Vice President's Suburban continued on—alone—down a concrete ramp that descended into the earth.

The car raced down a long subterranean concrete-walled tunnel.

It wasn't just long.

It was really, really long, and wide enough only for a single car. Fluorescent lights on its solid grey walls flashed by as they sped down it.

'What is this?' Trey asked.

The Vice President answered: 'Ever wondered why you never see the President or bigshot VIPs actually leaving an airport? This is why. Every major airport in the United States has a tunnel like this. It's called an E.C.I.: an Egress for Cleared Individuals. This one is about three miles long and passes under the main runways of LAX.'

'Where does it end?' Cassie asked.

'Here.'

The tunnel abruptly widened into a similarly concrete-walled space, only this was the size of a hall.

On one side of the space was the only exit: an elevator recessed into the thick sturdy wall.

Their Suburban pulled up in front of the elevator.

The Vice President got out—flanked by his personal Secret Service bodyguard, who clearly was not allowed to let the V.P. out of his sight—followed cautiously by Cassie and Trey.

The elevator's doors opened and the Vice President stepped inside it and invited them to join him. 'This way.'

They got in the elevator with the V.P. and his bodyguard.

They rode up in silence.

Then the Vice President spoke in his familiar Midwestern drawl.

'For three days, I've been praying to the Lord for guidance, for advice on how to navigate our way through this time when it came. Then God answered my prayers when I was informed that a special visitor had arrived off the coast of California and was waiting there . . .'

The elevator stopped and its doors began to open, revealing a large hangar, its massive doors closed.

The first thing Cassie saw in the hangar, parked inside it, was a large white-and-blue plane: *Air Force Two*, the Vice President's plane.

'. . . with a personal message for me. A personal *offer* for me.'

The elevator doors came fully open, to reveal—

—a lone man waiting for them.

He was about thirty.

Tall and muscular.

With high cheekbones and eerie yellow-rimmed eyes.

And dressed entirely in Kremlin red armour with a yellow hammer and sickle imprinted on it.

Cassie's breath caught in her throat.

'Oh, *fuck* . . .' Trey said.

Cassie couldn't believe it.

She had seen this man before, not in person, but in

the body-cam footage from Cobalt Green's rescue of the *Caribbean Star* cruise liner.

Standing right in front of her, not ten feet away, was the Fury's oldest son, the Fury of Moscow.

The Secret Service agent beside Cassie sprang into action.

He charged out of the elevator, drawing his gun, and fired it furiously and repeatedly at Moscow, only for his bullets to bounce harmlessly off the Russian superhuman.

Moscow snatched the pistol from the agent's two-fisted grip and with little apparent effort broke it in two with just his fingers and thumb.

Then he punched the Secret Service agent in the face with such force, he sent the man's nose and eyes fully three inches back into his head, creating a concave void in his skull. The agent collapsed on the spot, killed instantly.

Cassie threw a hand to her mouth.

Trey instinctively stepped in front of her.

The Vice President barely even blinked. He examined his fingernails as he stepped out of the elevator and joined the Fury of Moscow.

'That visitor was this gentleman,' he said, 'who was in a Russian Akula-class submarine that's been waiting off the coast since Cobalt died a week ago, waiting for today. Hello, Moskva.'

The Fury of Moscow grinned. 'Mr Vice President. So nice to see you again.'

When he spoke, he looked only at Cassie.

He scanned her up and down, assessing her, evaluating her.

'So this is the one. This is the natural daughter of Cobalt.'

His eyes, Cassie found herself noting, were far more frightening in real life than they had been on the body-cam footage. They radiated a lethal combination of intelligence and cunning.

Clenching her teeth, she turned to the Vice President. 'You slimy prick. You said he made you an offer. What was that offer?'

The Vice President said, 'That when this day was over, I would be the Fury's—how to put this—local governor here in America.'

'You mother*fucker*,' Cassie said. 'You sold us out!'

'I am *easing the transition*,' the Vice President said patiently. 'As the Fury and his sons take control of our nation and establish a new order in America, the transition won't be pleasant. But I am sure that with the help of the Lord, I will be able to make it less unpleasant for as many Americans as is realistically possible.'

Cassie glared at him. His ability to rationalise his

betrayal of his oath, his office, his country and his people was breathtaking.

Trey said, 'And what happens to the President? Your boss, your friend?'

The Vice President shrugged. 'When all the Cobalt children are dead, I will direct the Fury and his sons to the President's secret location and, after the Fury does what he desires to the President and the First Lady, the President will be executed. I was never really fond of him. He just needed me for the white evangelical vote.'

Cassie shook her head. 'You sold out your country, you two-faced sanctimonious bastard!'

'No, I didn't sell out the country,' the Vice President said calmly. 'Just *you*.'

Cassie's blood chilled.

Moscow smirked, seeing her get it. 'Young lady, the bargain I struck with the Vice President was simple: he was to draw you out of hiding and hand you over. Then we would give him whatever post he desired in our new America.'

'You're going to kill me?' Cassie said.

'Oh, no! *No, no, no*,' Moscow said. 'It's much worse than that. My father was very specific in his instructions. He wants you brought to him *alive*, so he can make you his most prized personal slave.'

As Moscow said this, Cassie heard a voice in her head, the voice of Cobalt Red during one of their fight sessions.

'*There are times when you gotta realise* that the fight has already started *and you'll need to throw the first punch.*'

This fight had already started.

What happened next happened very, very fast.

Cassie whipped around in a lightning-quick spinning high kick that connected with Moscow's chest and sent him flying forty feet across the hangar.

Moscow smashed into the forward landing gear of *Air Force Two*, hitting it with such force that he bent the landing gear's thick metal struts and the nose of the huge plane lurched downward, dropping five feet.

That kick would have made both Cobalt Red and Golden Gary proud. She'd struck first and the kick had been perfectly timed.

Moscow lay beneath the plane, dazed but not unconscious.

The Vice President gaped in shock.

Cassie rounded on him, grabbed him roughly by the tie and shoved him back into the open elevator. 'You're coming with us. When this is over, you're going to jail.'

'You don't have any proof!' the Vice President sneered as the doors closed and the elevator descended.

'Trey,' Cassie said. 'Were you recording?'

Trey extracted his cell phone from his pocket. The Voice Memos app was open and still recording.

'Always, baby,' he said.

The elevator opened onto the subterranean turn-around, where the Vice President's Suburban was still waiting with the engine running.

Seeing the three of them emerge at speed from the elevator, its driver got out and reached for his gun.

Cassie parried his gun and seized him by the neck, said, 'Sorry, buddy, but we don't have time to explain,' and then promptly banged his head against the hood of the car, knocking him out.

Then they were in the Suburban with Trey at the wheel and Cassie covering the Vice President. The big SUV peeled out of the turnaround and sped back into the long tunnel.

'Floor it!' Cassie yelled.

'You got it!' Trey called back and the walls of the tunnel became rushing grey blurs on either side of them.

And then—

—*bam!*—

—Moscow appeared behind the fleeing car, flying fast, and he grabbed it by its rear bumper, picked up its rear wheels and . . . flipped it.

The big black Suburban, already travelling at breakneck speed, rolled wildly and began tumbling down the tight concrete-walled space.

Trey was wearing a seatbelt.

Cassie and the Vice President weren't. But she reacted faster, bracing herself against the ceiling.

The V.P. didn't. He screamed as he banged and bounced all over the interior of the rolling, crashing car.

The roll concluded with a metallic bang as the black Suburban ended up on its roof, upside down, almost exactly halfway down the length of the tunnel.

The Fury of Moscow strode down the tunnel toward the crashed SUV, its wheels still spinning uselessly.

'You okay?' Cassie asked Trey.

He was bleeding from a cut to his forehead but he nodded. 'Yeah.'

Beside him, the Vice President groaned. His face was completely covered in cuts, blood and wounds. He'd probably broken a few bones, too, Cassie figured.

She dragged Trey out of the crashed car and pushed him further down the tunnel, toward the exit.

'Go,' she said. 'Run. As fast as you can. I'll catch up.'

Trey didn't argue. He took off down the tunnel.

Cassie eyed the Fury of Moscow.

He returned her gaze from the other side of the crashed Suburban.

'You got lucky with that kick,' he said. 'You won't get another chance to do that. Still, I won't kill you. I told you I must bring you to my father alive.'

Cassie's eyes flicked from Moscow to the upside-down Suburban and the pathetic figure of the Vice President still lying inside it, bloodied and broken.

Moscow was right. She wouldn't get another chance to unleash the first punch. He was too smart for that. And in a stand-up fight, with all his battle-hardened skills, he'd probably beat her.

Cassie bit her lip.

'Well,' she said. 'The world had to find out eventually.'

And then she did it.

Did something no-one, not even Trey, had seen her do.

She flew.

But at first she didn't fly far.

She flew up, straight up, into the concrete ceiling of the tunnel directly above the crashed Suburban . . .

. . . where she *punched* the ceiling with all her considerable strength.

The ceiling cracked instantly.

Then, flying quickly away from Moscow, Cassie did it again and again, punching the ceiling at twenty-foot intervals down the tunnel.

Moscow realised what she had done too late.

'Damn it, no . . .' he breathed as the first ominous groan came from above him.

The ceiling—buried underneath two hundred feet of earth and cement—began to break out in hundreds of splintering cracks until suddenly it gave way and collapsed catastrophically.

★ ★ ★

It would be the last thing the Vice President of the United States ever saw.

From where he lay bleeding and dying inside the upside-down Suburban, he could see the grey ceiling through the windshield.

He saw it break out in the final series of spiderwebbing cracks and he knew then that it was going to come crashing down.

For a fleeting instant, he thought about praying, but in the end all he could do was scream as untold tons of earth and cement caved in on the tunnel, crushing the Vice President of the United States—and the Suburban that contained him—in a single shocking instant.

Cassie watched it all from further down the tunnel.

Because of her blows, the roof had collapsed, filling the tunnel with perhaps a hundred yards of solid earth and concrete.

This had the effect—just as Cassie had hoped—of separating her from Moscow. That hundred yards of earth and concrete now lay between her and him.

Cassie waited a few moments to see if Moscow could break through it, but nothing happened.

She flew down the tunnel to rejoin Trey.

'So,' he said. 'You can fly, huh?'

'It was—I didn't think—I wasn't sure I should tell you . . .' Cassie stammered.

'Babe. I don't care that you kept it a secret from me. You're even more awesome than I thought!'

'Thanks,' she said. 'Come on, then. We gotta get out of here.'

With those words, she picked him up and flew him at phenomenal speed down the rest of the tunnel.

After zooming past the other vehicles of the Vice President's motorcade outside, they found a car in a nearby rental lot with the keys inside it. To keep flying was to risk getting spotted.

With their eyes searching the sky for the Fury of Moscow, they drove away.

Cassie and Trey's car skidded to a halt outside their house.

They sprang out of it and hurried up the walk.

'Jesus Christ, that was intense,' Trey said. 'This whole day has been crazy.'

'Crazy,' Cassie repeated, looking sideways at him. 'No-one anticipates crazy . . .'

'What are you thinking?'

Cassie paused at the front door, gazing hard at her husband.

'I'm thinking Moscow is already here, his dad is on the way and two of his brothers are coming in from Hawaii. I'm thinking we need a plan, one that might include a little crazy—'

She unlocked the door and pushed it open—

—to find someone in their living room, waiting for them.

Cobalt Black. Lounging on their sofa.

'Be careful what you wish for,' he said.

Cassie and Trey stepped into their living room.

They moved slowly, cautiously, their eyes on Cobalt Black, like people skirting a wild animal.

Cassie walked up to Black, scanning the floor at his feet for hologram discs.

'You really here, Blaine?' she said.

Black extended his hand . . .

. . . and Cassie took it. They shook.

'Not a hologram,' Black said. 'You know what they say, desperate times.'

Cobalt Black stood and started pacing, unable as ever to sit still.

'We don't have much time,' Cassie said. 'Did you bust out of your prison lab?'

'Busted out or was let out?' Black shrugged. 'We need to talk, you and me—about being a hero or not.'

'I told you my reasons for—'

'I don't care about your reasons—I know your reasons—I know every thought you can have before you have it. Do you have any idea how hard it is for me, waiting for people to catch up? Jesus.'

He cut himself off, took a deep, calming breath.

Then he continued. 'The question, dear sister, is not why be a goodie-goodie superhero like our mother. The question is *why be good at all*?'

Cassie frowned. 'What?'

Black said, 'When she got her powers, Mother dearest took on a role. America's hero. She subsumed herself for the common good.'

'Yes, for her fellow Americans—'

'It was stupid.'

'Because she cared for more than just herself?'

'No, it was stupid based on first principles. Why defend these people at all? Why serve a government? Why serve *anyone*? We should *be* the government! If we can dispense justice and might, why don't we?'

'Can you hear yourself?' Cassie said.

'America is leaving us for dead! Look at what happened to Red in Chicago. *They disowned him!* They're cutting us loose. Let's cut them loose and do a deal with the Fury.'

'A deal?'

'Or . . . if you and I beat the Fury together, we claim this country as our rightful reward,' Cobalt Black said.

'Blaine, you can't be serious—'

'One-time offer—if you help me kill him, I let you rule

America with me. If you don't and I kill him by myself, I leave you behind and rule alone and probably-eventually-kill-you-to-make-sure-you're-not-a-threat-to-my-rule.'

Trey said, 'You really are insane.'

'*Wait*,' Cassie said. 'You think you can kill him?'

'Yes.'

'How?'

'Shock and awe and a big, big bang.'

'Why did you come here, Blaine?'

That stopped him. He blinked weirdly, tic-like, his brain working too fast. Trey was right. He really was insane.

But when he answered, Black almost sounded sad, forlorn. 'I just wanted to . . . talk with someone who would get it. I struggle to find equal conversational partners, you know, and you're, well, almost good enough. One-time offer?'

'No way,' Cassie said flatly.

'Then I have somewhere to be.'

And with those words, Black left.

Cassie and Trey exchanged worried looks.

'What the hell was that?' Trey said.

'Come on. Whatever he's doing, we need to have our own plan. Like my dad said.'

▰▰▰ DAD II ▰▰▰

DILLON, MONTANA
9 MONTHS AGO

Cassie watched them from the kitchen. It was a touching sight.

America's greatest hero—strong, fast, more powerful than anyone in the entire country—tending to her husband.

Cassie's dad lay in his favourite armchair, wrapped in a blanket, while Cobalt gently adjusted it.

He coughed—a deep, hacking cough. His health had been deteriorating for some time now.

'Admit it,' he said weakly, 'it's hard being married to such a strong and powerful man, isn't it?'

Christine Cobalt tenderly touched his face.

'There's no-one else I'd rather be married to, Arnold Cobalt.'

'And my surname did make for a kinda badass super-hero name.'

'Sure did, stud.'

'God, Christine, do you remember when you got pregnant and we stayed out of sight?'

Christine Cobalt joined Cassie in the adjoining kitchen, helping her with the tray of tea and crackers she'd been preparing.

'Oh, I remember,' she called out to her husband.

He laughed. ''Course, it was different back then, before social media. We managed to keep your mother out of public view for the few months she had the baby bump.'

Cassie said, 'I'm glad the Fury didn't attack then.'

Her mother laughed. 'I mighta been pregnant but I was so ragingly hormonal, I coulda taken him.'

Dad said, 'Then we kept *you* out of sight, Cassie. For years. Did all sorts of things, didn't we, hon?'

'It was a team effort, baby,' Christine Cobalt said.

In the kitchen, she gave Cassie a warm smile.

Cassie's dad was still talking in the living room.

'Remember that, Cassie, as you live your life with your nice husband. That's the key to a successful marriage: *you're a team*. The other key is . . .' He trailed off.

Cassie picked up the tea tray and stepped out of the kitchen into the living room.

'Yeah,' she said, 'what's the other—?'

She stopped in mid-stride.

Her father lay still in his chair, his head tilted back, the life gone out of him.

He was dead.

Christine Cobalt rushed to her husband's side while Cassie just stood there in the entryway to the kitchen, dumbly holding the tray, numb and speechless.

'We've got maybe two hours till the Fury and his other boys get to L.A.,' Cassie said as she and Trey hurried around the house, grabbing things. 'Can you get my security pass? It's on the dresser.'

'On it.' Trey dashed into their bedroom.

Cassie pulled out her cell phone. 'I gotta call Gary in Vegas.'

She dialled: GG.

Ring-ring . . .

Ring-ring . . .

No answer.

THE STRIP, LAS VEGAS
TODAY

Cobalt Gold stood out in the middle of Las Vegas Boulevard, or as it was more commonly known, the Strip.

Normally, the Strip bustled with the unique energy of Las Vegas.

Today it was deserted.

Like the rest of America, the people of Vegas were hiding in their homes and hotel rooms, watching their nation get attacked.

The Fury of Russia stood a short distance away from Golden Gary, facing him.

'Finally,' the Fury said. 'Cobalt Gold. The decadent one. The one who worships at the altar of Sodom.'

Golden Gary shook his head. 'Or just *gay*.'

The Fury scanned Las Vegas.

'America,' he said. 'For all your petty puritanism, all your talk of values, you still have this place.'

'Vegas, baby,' Gary said.

'You have a reputation as a fighter,' the Fury said.

'Maybe.'

'Welcome to the fight of your life.'

And with a roar, the Fury rushed at Golden Gary.

In Cassie's living room, as she and Trey hurriedly gathered their stuff, the smart speaker played a news report:

'We're getting word from Las Vegas that the Fury of Russia is fighting Cobalt Gold—'

Cassie froze.

'Oh, god, Gary . . .'

■■■■■■ GOLDEN GARY ■■■■■

PLANET HOLLYWOOD, LAS VEGAS
2 YEARS AGO

Cassie sat in the vast penthouse suite of Planet Hollywood, forty storeys above the lights of Vegas.

The suite occupied the entire top floor of the casino–hotel and was basically Gary's home, a thank-you gift from the casino companies for keeping their city safe. Cassie had come up via a secret back elevator.

Gary brought her a cocktail from his private bar and sat down with her.

'A toast!' he said. 'To us! The two best-looking super-heroes in America, even if nobody knows you're one.'

Cassie clinked glasses and took a sip.

'I saw the whole song thing on social media,' she said.

'I stand by what I said: it's the best song ever written,' Gary said.

'The *Baywatch* theme song?'

'Listen to the lyrics. It's about telling people you're watching over them, that you stand at the ready, that it's going to be all right. Hero stuff. Something to remember when *you* decide to come out of the hero closet.'

'Twitter was brutal on you.'

'Never acknowledge the haters,' Gary said. 'Who cares what someone with three followers thinks? I got *twelve million*.'

Golden Gary leapt from his seat.

'Oh, speaking of coming out of the closet.'

He raced out of the room and returned a moment later carrying a large flat box.

He presented it to Cassie.

'For when you emerge from the chrysalis like the butterfly you are.'

Cassie opened the flat box to reveal . . .

. . . a blue-and-white superhero suit. It was spectacular.

Sleek.

Feminine but strong.

White leather with deep blue racing stripes on one side.

Matching helmet, too.

Cassie gasped. 'Gary, it's beautiful. But does it—'

'It fits,' Gary said. 'I stole a peek at your measurements last time I swung by your place. Got my guy to build it for you. Theatre guy. Does Cirque du Soleil. Go on, put it on.'

Cassie stepped into the next room to do so. As she did, Gary called out: 'It's a Kevlar bi-weave with poly-ceramic threading. It'll withstand fire, most blades and deflect a bullet. Although, can your skin withstand a gunshot?'

'Don't know. Never tried,' Cassie said from the other room.

Gary shrugged. 'Funny, bullets just bounce off me . . .'

He fell silent as Cassie re-entered, dressed in her new suit.

'Whoa,' he said. 'Mother-pumpkin . . .'

Cassie was suddenly unsure. 'What? Is it no good?'

Golden Gary shook his head. 'Honey, it's *insanely* good. We're lucky you went underground 'cause you would be the most smokin' superhero chick on the planet if you ever went public.'

Cassie wriggled a little. 'It pinches a bit on my boobs.'

'The price of hotness, hotness.'

Cassie checked herself in a mirror. She did look kinda good in it.

Golden Gary stepped up behind her, also looking in the mirror.

'You're a hero,' he said.

'I don't know about that—'

'You can't hide a light like yours,' Gary said. 'If you ever want to be her, you're Cobalt Blue.'

LAS VEGAS
TODAY

Golden Gary had more than just a reputation as a fighter.

He was actually the *best* fighter of all the Cobalts—and a true student of the art of fighting.

(Cobalt Green did his fight training in the Army while Cobalt Red learned his skills at the Chicago P.D. At the age of eight, Cobalt Black spurned Gary's offer to teach him saying that, frankly, he thought he could teach himself much better.)

When it came to Cassie, Gary was keenly aware of her sessions with Cobalt Red and what they meant to both Red and Cassie, so he made sure not to undermine that.

But knowing that Red's techniques were more practical and streetwise, with Red's permission, Gary had given Cassie formal instruction in kickboxing and jiu-jitsu: the former for long-range attacking moves and the latter for grappling and joint locks.

In short, Golden Gary wasn't just any fighter.

Cobalt Gold was the fighter of fighters.

His battle with the Fury was nothing short of epic, by far the longest of the one-on-one duels the Russian had fought that day.

It lasted for thirty minutes, with Gary and the Fury trading blows as they whipped between the gaudy collection of buildings that form the Vegas skyline.

Gary used every skill he had, every evasive move, every brilliant attack.

At one point, sweeping around the new Sphere concert hall, he unleashed a scintillating sequence of punches that—amazingly—*cracked* the Fury's red-tinted visor.

Then he flung the distracted Fury right into the Sphere, causing the whole massive globe to come free of its mounts and roll into the grassy golf course next door, only for the Fury to spring out of the wreckage, grab Gary, and with a roar hurl him right through the 550-feet-tall Ferris wheel beside the LINQ casino, causing the whole Ferris wheel to topple while Gary went tumbling into a deep construction pit near it.

And that was when the Fury did it.

With Gary temporarily down, the Russian flew to the end of the Strip and, using his mighty strength, *wrenched* the Stratosphere Tower—the iconic needle-shaped tower that has long been the centrepiece of the Vegas skyline, all eighty storeys of it—out of the ground.

Then, flying high above the city, he raised it above his head in both hands and hurled it like a giant spear *into the pit at Golden Gary.*

Gary's eyes boggled at the sight.

The building rushed downward at him, eighty storeys of it disappearing into the pit at speed.

A colossal impact followed.

A super-gigantic dust cloud billowed out of the pit.

The Fury hovered above the site, searching for any sign of Golden Gary.

No movement.

Nothing.

There was no way anyone could have survived such a blow, such a titanic, colossal, thunderous blow.

The Fury stared into the pit, at the gigantic crumpled tower lying in it.

'You fought the best of all your siblings. And died honourably.'

The Fury then tipped the Bellagio hotel–casino into its lake, dropped the MGM Grand onto Caesar's Palace, and speared the Strip's giant Eiffel Tower replica into the runway of Harry Reid International Airport, leaving it embedded upside down in the tarmac.

Then he flew off, heading ever westward.

The smart speaker in Cassie's kitchen delivered the news.

'. . . *Cobalt Gold is dead. Killed by the Fury of Russia moments ago in Las Vegas when he threw a building on him.*'

Cassie emerged from her bedroom, stopping as she heard the news.

Then her phone rang. She grabbed it.

'Hello?'

Cobalt Black's voice said, 'Last chance to join me.'

'What have you done, Blaine?' Cassie said.

'Last chance.'

'You know I can't,' Cassie said.

GROOM LAKE MILITARY TESTING COMPLEX (RESTRICTED ACCESS), NEVADA TODAY

Cobalt Black stood alone on a military runway in the Nevada desert, cell phone to his ear.

The high-security base on which he stood and in which he had lived and worked for the last ten years was about forty miles northwest of Las Vegas.

People in the Air Force and other branches of the military called it the Groom Lake Military Testing Complex. Regular people and conspiracy theorists knew it by its old designation: Area 51.

The tarmac beside Black stretched away toward the vast salt lake that surrounded the base. It shimmered in the heat haze. A dozen huge aircraft hangars surrounded Cobalt Black.

'Your emotions make you weak, sister,' he said into the phone before hanging up on Cassie.

Then he looked up at the sky.

'Hello there,' he said.

The Fury of Russia hovered in the air above him.

'The brilliant one,' the Fury said.

Black shrugged. 'Welcome to Groom Lake. Strategic weapons centre. Nukes, chem, bio. All the good stuff. We need to talk.'

The Fury landed in front of him.

'Speak.'

'Two options,' Black said. 'One: we join forces and you give me America to rule.'

'And Option Two?' the Fury said.

'I kill you and rule America anyway.'

'And how exactly would you do that?' the Fury asked, intrigued.

'You can withstand a nuclear blast, right?'

'Yes.'

'How about ten of them?'

The Fury frowned at that, suddenly concerned. He glanced at all the hangars around him, as if seeing them for the first time.

'I wanted to do this in a city,' Black said, lifting up a remote control . . .

. . . as his entire body flickered.

The Fury blinked in surprise as he saw the small silver disc on the ground.

Black wasn't there.

He was a hologram.

The Fury spun as—

—all ten hangars around him blasted apart—

—and the entire base blew up with ten simultaneous nuclear explosions.

The ten white-hot mega-sized blasts completely engulfed the Fury before rising into the stratosphere as a ring of mushroom clouds, clouds that soon became one super-colossal pillar of smoke.

And from a hill ten miles away, Cobalt Black watched it.

He grinned thinly . . .

. . . but a moment later, his smile faded as . . .

. . . the tiny figure of the Fury zoomed up out of the very top of the gargantuan mushroom cloud like a thin red laser beam, shooting into the upper stratosphere, *outrunning* the rising blast.

'Damn.' Cobalt Black scowled.

Then he turned and swept away.

LOS ANGELES
TODAY

Cassie hurried into her bedroom, threw open her closet and pulled from it the big flat box that Golden Gary had given her in Vegas two years previously.

On the smart speaker, the newsreader said, '*With Cobalt Gold dead, authorities are wondering what the Fury will do. He appears to be heading west toward Los Angeles.*'

Cassie stared at the box.

Then she opened it, revealing the suit.

Her suit.

Minutes later, she was wearing it.

White leather, blue racing stripes, form fitted.

Holding her white helmet under her arm, Cassie went into the kitchen and to the fridge, to the set of coloured Sharpies dangling off it.

She grabbed the green Sharpie and made a mark with it on the back of her helmet.

Cobalt Green's voice echoed in her mind:

'The best place to fight a battle is on home turf.'

Then she made a red mark. Red's voice:

'To know you can take a punch and keep going.'

A purple mark. Purple:

'You work hard, Cassie. You stick at things.'

White's voice:

'And you're so clever.'

Silver's voice:

'You have two things Black doesn't. Imagination and the humility to listen to other people's ideas. If anyone can figure the Fury out, it's you.'

Her dad's voice:

'Crazy can win against the odds . . . I played crazy.'

Lastly, Cassie slashed a yellow mark on her helmet as she heard Golden Gary's voice:

'You're a hero . . . If you ever want to be her, you're Cobalt Blue.'

When she was done, Cassie had made a row of coloured marks on her white helmet, marks that represented everyone she loved, her father and all her siblings.

She was, she now realised, the combination of them all.

Then in her mind she heard one final voice.

That of her mother, Christine Cobalt.

'It'll all come down to you.'

Cassie put on her helmet.

And her game face.

THE SUIT

Cassie jumped into her car. Trey was already at the wheel.

'Nice outfit. Where to, superhero?'

Cassie stared straight ahead, her eyes focused.

'Home turf.'

Forty minutes later, Trey dropped Cassie off at SpaceX headquarters near Long Beach.

The huge warehouses of the famed rocket company stood alongside the broad concrete trench that is the Los Angeles River.

Cassie got out.

'Go,' she said. 'I'll meet you at the Seventh Street Bridge.'

'Seventh Street Bridge, got it,' Trey said. 'You sure about this?'

Cassie nodded. 'I have to draw them to me. I have to be the bait.'

'This is crazy, you know,' Trey said.

'I know,' Cassie said. 'But that's how you beat a guy like him.'

Trey sped away from Long Beach, heading north parallel to the concrete river, back toward downtown. It was a quick drive since the roads were largely empty.

Just as he arrived at his destination and pulled to a stop, a red human-shaped figure appeared above the mountains to the east of L.A. and streaked across the sky, zooming like a laser toward the skyscrapers of downtown.

The Fury of Russia had arrived in Los Angeles.

Minutes later, high above the towers of L.A., the Fury was met by his eldest son, the Fury of Moscow, and then by two other flying red streaks that came in from the west, from over the Pacific Ocean: his other two sons, the Furies of Stalingrad and Leningrad.

Floating above the skyscrapers, above the limitless sprawl of L.A., the four superpowered Russians scanned the city in every direction.

Then they heard it.

Distantly at first.

Beats of music. Iconic beats. 1980s beats.

The *Baywatch* theme song.

The Fury listened, his super-sensitive ears zeroing in on the source of the song.

Long Beach.

And a warehouse there, on the roof of which he saw a figure dressed in white and blue.

Cassie.

She was staring right back at him.

'There,' the Fury growled.

He and his three sons flew toward her.

Cassie hurried inside.

Not long after, the four Russian supermen landed on all four sides of the main SpaceX warehouse, surrounding it.

They went in, searching, hunting.

The Fury himself entered via the main reception area, his eyes scanning left and right.

The Fury of Stalingrad advanced down a hallway.

The Fury of Moscow peered into an office.

The Fury of Leningrad stepped into a darkened lab.

He was crossing the wide dark room when a woman's voice spoke from the darkness: 'Looking for me?'

He spun . . . and saw her . . . on the other side of the gloom, took a step that way—

Gloop.

—and dropped knee-deep into a thick, white and extremely cold liquid of some sort.

'Ah!' Leningrad shouted.

He looked down.

He was standing in a vat of some kind, filled with supercooled liquid nitrogen that gripped his legs tightly.

Then he looked up to see . . .

. . . Cassie, barely ten yards away, her eyes level with his.

Oddly, her legs were bent, so that she was in a kneeling position.

The thing was: she wasn't kneeling on the ground.

She was hovering.

In the air, a couple of inches above the pool of liquid nitrogen.

With her legs bent, it had appeared that she was standing on solid ground, and in this way, she'd lured the Fury of Leningrad to step forward into the vat.

'Welcome to America,' she said, hitting a switch beside her.

Something whirred in the darkness, powering up.

Then a sequence of green LEDs sprang to life like runway lights . . .

. . . and in their soft glow Leningrad saw a set of electromagnetic rail tracks aimed right at him . . .

. . . just as Cassie placed a metal bolt on those tracks and released it.

The bolt whizzed down the electromagnetic rail, shockingly fast, and slammed into Leningrad's chest.

His eyes sprang wide.

There was now a small hole through his body. The bolt—travelling at almost the fastest speed man was capable of generating—had penetrated his superskin and gone right through his heart.

He was dead, but he was still standing up.

Only then did the Fury of Leningrad collapse into the liquid nitrogen, face-down. Dead.

A door banged open on the other side of the broad room.

The Fury and his other two sons burst through it into the Rocket Fuel Facility.

The Fury looked from his dead son in the vat over to Cassie as she flew out the rear door.

'Get her!' he yelled.

PURSUIT OVER THE L.A. RIVER

Cassie shot out of SpaceX like a bullet out of a gun, flying fast and low, leaving a blue-edged vapour trail behind her as she banked at speed into the wide concrete trench that was the L.A. River.

She shot north up the river.

Two seconds later, the Fury of Stalingrad and his older brother, the Fury of Moscow, came zooming out of SpaceX after her, also flying superfast, trailing red streaks behind them.

Cassie flew at unbelievable speed, close to three hundred miles per hour.

She rocketed north up the L.A. River, heading toward Downtown, zooming under bridges, banking left, sweeping right, doing rolling loops as the slanted walls of the trench swept by her in blurs on either side.

The two young Furies raced after her, with Stalingrad ahead of Moscow.

The Fury of Russia rose up into the sky behind them, watching the pursuit.

From where he was, he could see the river stretching northward through the industrial neighbourhoods of L.A., with the three tiny figures streaking up it—the blue one chased by the two red ones—bending and weaving under the cross-bridges.

Cassie flew with her face set.

She was flying so damned fast it was almost too much to absorb.

She swept under a bridge, narrowly missing its concrete pillars, with the two Fury boys close behind her.

Banking with the course of the river, under more bridges, rolling left, sweeping right.

The Fury of Stalingrad was close now, about three hundred yards ahead of his brother.

Cassie saw the Seventh Street Bridge up ahead, spotted a small concrete side-tunnel below it to the left—

—and banked that way, whipping into the side tunnel, where she shot into darkness—

—passing Trey who was waiting in there—

—and who immediately ignited two J.P.L. cutting lasers behind her, angling their superthin iridescent red beams diagonally across the width of the tunnel, creating a deadly glowing X.

A second later, Stalingrad roared into the tunnel at phenomenal speed—

—and flew right through the cutting lasers.

The lasers scythed through him, tearing him apart, cutting him in an X lengthways down his body.

The pieces of his corpse slid to fleshy halts on the concrete floor of the tunnel like slabs of meat.

'Ew,' Trey said, turning up his nose.

Cassie yanked him away. 'Go. You can't stay here.'

She pushed him deeper into the darkness of the tunnel, looking anxiously back at its mouth.

A moment later, the Fury of Moscow and the Fury himself arrived in the mouth of the tunnel . . .

. . . to find the tunnel empty.

No Cassie.

The Fury and his eldest son saw the X-shaped laser and Stalingrad's dead body.

'She's laying traps for us,' Moscow said.

'She's clever,' the Fury said. 'Like her mother.'

They stepped under the crisscrossing laser beams, looking down at the split-open corpse of Stalingrad.

Which was why they never saw the figure descending silently and smoothly out of a manhole shaft above them.

It was Cassie. Flying.

Very slowly.

Without a sound.

Head-down, feet in the air, directly over the Fury.

'I hate clever,' the Fury said.

Cassie was right over him now *and he didn't know it.*

So close. Frighteningly close.

She reached her hands down on either side of his masked face . . . her fingers spreading wide . . . to grab his mask . . .

. . . when the Fury cocked his head, smelling something, sensing something.

His eyes narrowed.

And he spun suddenly and snatched Cassie's right hand and threw her to the ground.

'What do you think you're doing?!' he roared.

Cassie leapt to her feet as the Fury advanced on her and swung one of his mighty fists.

For Cassie, the world went slow, and as she saw the Fury pull his right fist back, she heard in her mind the voice of her brother, Cobalt Red:

'Read the punch before it comes.'

The Fury unleashed the punch.

Cassie ducked left. The blow missed.

Then Moscow swung.

Cassie bobbed right then punched him square in the nose. Dropped him.

The Fury attacked her again, a flurry of blows that she managed to avoid.

And then a punch landed.

It was so strong, Cassie's visor cracked and she recoiled, a shrill ringing filling her head.

She blinked hard, trying to focus.

Red's voice: '*If you get hit in a fight, you gotta keep your wits long enough to avoid the killer blow that's comin' in next.*'

The Fury bellowed with rage as he lunged forward with the killer blow—as Cassie blinked back to her senses and dived desperately out of the way—and the blow missed by millimetres and the Fury overbalanced.

And Cassie sprang up and . . .

. . . yanked his carbon-ceramic facemask off his helmet!

With a loud crack, the facemask came free of the Fury and before he could even react, Cassie flew into a round side pipe in the darkness, superquick and suddenly gone.

The Fury whirled around, roaring with anger.

He touched his exposed face.

'She thinks she can kill me . . .' he said slowly.

Then, shouting: 'DO YOU THINK YOU CAN DO THAT, CHILD? DO YOU HONESTLY BELIEVE YOU CAN KILL ME?!'

Cassie emerged from the maze of sewers about half a mile away, where she found Trey waiting for her as planned.

She climbed out from a manhole and hugged him.

She still wore her half-broken helmet and held in one hand the Fury's facemask.

'Got it.'

'Next stop?' Trey asked.

'My home turf,' Cassie said. 'But we need him to see us go. Hop on.'

Trey jumped onto her back and they flew off.

The Fury and Moscow stepped out into the L.A. River in time to see Cassie and Trey fly off toward some industrial warehouses near Downtown.

The Fury ground his teeth in anger.

Then, with a powerful boom, he shot off into the air after them, his eldest son following close behind.

J.P.L. FACILITY
DOWNTOWN L.A.

Cassie and Trey landed outside J.P.L.'s warehouse facility near Downtown and hurried inside.

Moments later, the Fury and his son arrived.

'Another trap?' Moscow said.

'Undoubtedly,' the Fury said.

They went in anyway.

They moved through the empty complex, bathed in darkness.

The Fury sniffed the air. 'That way,' he said.

They entered a strange-looking room, one with nozzles on the walls.

The Fury of Moscow approached one of the nozzles and touched it, curious.

He didn't know Cassie was watching him from the adjoining observation room, waiting for him to get close to the nozzle.

She slammed her finger down on a switch—

—and a jet of gaseous nitrogen sprayed right into Moscow's face, blasting straight down his throat.

The Fury spun. 'Close your mouth! Don't let it—'

But it was too late.

The Fury of Moscow gagged, clutching his throat, his face going white.

He dropped to his knees as Cassie's voice came in over the intercom: 'Welcome to the Cold Space Lab. This chamber mimics space. That gas is minus 200 degrees. Your lungs are snap-freezing.'

The Fury looked from his dying son to Cassie behind the glass of the observation room.

Moscow writhed on the floor and went still.

'Yours will freeze, too, asshole,' Cassie said.

The Fury was gazing at his dead son. He seemed disappointed more than anything.

'My sons have half my strength,' he said softly. 'Your gas won't affect me. My country tested such things on me. So now it is you and me, and I am twice the hero you are.'

Cassie saw that he was right—the gas wasn't affecting him. She raced out the back door of the observation room a moment before the Fury came bursting through the glass, shattering it.

★ ★ ★

Cassie ran full-tilt through the corridors and hallways of J.P.L., even flew down some of them.

Her plan a failure, she fled into a large satellite-construction hall, running for her life, when she was suddenly bowled over from behind by the flying Fury and they crashed to the floor.

He ended up astride her.

Ripped off her half-broken helmet.

Backhanded her.

Again, the ringing in her ears.

He hit her again.

Dazed, concussed and on the verge of blacking out, Cassie tasted blood between her teeth.

The Fury glared down at her, pinned beneath him.

'The natural daughter of Cobalt. You've never bled from a wound, have you? Never been hit by anyone strong enough to break your superskin.'

He leaned in close and sniffed her lasciviously. 'I can smell your fear. You reek of it.'

Cassie struggled beneath him. 'I'm not afraid of you. You won't win.'

'Oh, I will win. And you will see me win. I will beat you into subservience, put a rope around your throat, and make you my personal slave, my sexual playthi—'

Whack!

A steel pole slammed into the back of the Fury's

head, wielded by—

—Trey.

'Get away from my wife, douchebag,' he said.

Unfortunately, the blow didn't hurt the Fury at all. It only served to break the pole.

The Fury slowly stood and turned. 'The husband. Brave. Also foolish.'

He stepped off Cassie and faced Trey.

Trey didn't back down.

'I could kill you with a single punch, little man,' the Fury said.

'I said, get away from my wife,' Trey replied.

Cassie groaned, still on the ground, and too far away to save Trey.

'No!' she gasped.

The Fury jabbed Trey in the chest with his index finger. Bones broke.

And Trey crumpled to the ground, wheezing, trying desperately to breathe.

The Fury stood over him.

'I will kill you like an insect—' he said.

When suddenly someone yanked the Fury from behind, pulling him away from the defenceless Trey.

'You couldn't kill me with a whole fucking building, you ugly piece of shit,' that someone said.

Standing there in the hall was Golden Gary.

★ ★ ★

Cassie didn't have time to process how Gary had managed to come back from the dead.

She just watched in surprise as he punched the shocked Fury, knocking him sideways.

Cassie was on her feet in a second and, seeing the Fury off balance, side-kicked him across the room.

Gary nodded to her. 'Hey, hotness. Golden Gary's in da house.'

Cassie saw Trey on the ground, unmoving. 'Trey!'

But Gary grabbed her arm. 'We can come back for him later if we survive this. Move!'

Gary hauled Cassie through a side door while the Fury was down.

Seconds later, they arrived in an empty corridor.

Cassie said, 'I thought he threw a building on you and killed you.'

Gary said, 'At the bottom of that pit was a sewer outlet. Flew out through it just in time. Came straight here to help you.'

'Well, I'm out of traps and ideas,' Cassie said.

'There's absolutely nothing else?' Gary asked.

Cassie thought for a moment. 'Maybe . . .'

Gary said, 'Kid, whatever it is, do it. I'll hold him off.'

'Gary, you can't beat him—'

'I know. But I can give you time.'

Cassie tenderly touched Gary's cheek and ran off.

Gary remained in the corridor.

He cracked his neck as he eyed the door leading back to the hall.

After a long moment, the door opened.

The Fury of Russia filled the doorway.

'So, the sodomite returns,' he said.

'Sodomite? Really? Your country has a very delightful gay scene, you know.'

The Fury flexed his knuckles. 'Ready?'

'Bring it,' Gary said.

The Fury rushed at Gary . . .

. . . and the fight began.

This time, Golden Gary knew what was coming and he fought awesomely. Fast punches. Quick dodges. Smaller and more nimble, he outmanoeuvred the Fury and was even looking like winning—

—until the Fury blocked a blow and punched him so hard that Gary smashed back into a wall, flying right through it, before he lay still, not moving.

With a grunt, the Fury stalked off in the direction Cassie had gone.

The Fury entered a very dark room. An array of blinking lights flashed and winked around him.

Clang!

The thick iron door behind him slammed shut, closed by Cassie, who was now standing behind the Fury, inside the dark room with him.

Looming over her, almost twice her size, the Fury took in the room around them: thick walls, a yellow-and-black sign on the door.

'What is this?' he said. 'A final lure? One last subterfuge?'

Cassie turned a dial on the wall. 'Just you and me,' she said.

A digital counter beside the dial ticked upward in rapid increments: in a matter of seconds **3** became **15** . . . then **30** . . . then **60** . . .

A low droning began to fill the air.

The Fury heard it.

'There is nothing you can do to hurt me. My bones are like steel. My skin is invulnerable.'

'I know about your skin,' Cassie said. 'It's actually a weakness, but not your biggest one.'

'And what is that?'

'You're used to winning.'

The Fury laughed. 'It's so hard when one cannot lose.'

'Tell me, can you still smell my fear?' Cassie asked him.

As she said this, she surreptitiously exhaled, expelling all the air from her lungs . . .

. . . while the Fury raised his nose and took a deep inhale, trying to smell.

Cassie eyed the counter. The numbers kept climbing: 70 . . . 75 . . . 80.

Then the signs nearby: DANGER: PRESSURISED ENVIRONMENT! and DECOMPRESSION RULES IN EFFECT.

They were in the high-pressure test chamber, designed to replicate the extreme pressure of Jupiter's atmosphere.

The counter hit 90.

Ninety atmospheres of pressure.

Cassie was standing beside her spherical metal satellite.

And in one swift move she pulled the EMERGENCY RELEASE handle on the heavy door behind her and . . .

. . . dived inside the hollow satellite, shutting herself inside it as . . .

. . . the thick pressure door sprang open!

★ ★ ★

The reaction was instantaneous.

An instant tornado filled the chamber. Air rushed out.

Loose paper whipped every which way.

Sirens wailed.

Emergency lights spun.

And warning screens blared: CHAMBER PRESSURE LOST — CHAMBER PRESSURE LOST.

The numbers of the counter whizzed downward at shocking speed.

A sudden, massive, catastrophic pressure drop.

And abruptly the Fury convulsed violently as something inside his chest exploded.

It made a truly disgusting sound.

And then a black bloody substance was ejected from his mouth, from deep within him, and the Fury doubled over in apparent pain.

The rush of air stopped.

Paper fluttered to the floor.

And the Fury of Russia collapsed to his knees, genuinely hurt.

He gasped. Coughed.

Cassie emerged from inside the metal satellite, perfectly fine.

She eyed the kneeling figure of the Fury warily.

The Fury gurgled up more lumpy black blood.

'What—what is this?'

Cassie stood over him. 'You just inhaled at ninety atmospheres of pressure.'

He glared at her, enraged, tried to stand, but instead toppled over pathetically onto his belly.

'And your invulnerable skin,' Cassie added, '*just kept in* nine hundred times your lungs' usual volume. Your lungs just exploded and because of your skin, the expanding air blew apart every organ in your chest cavity, including your heart. You just vomited it up.'

The Fury seemed confused. 'No-one can beat me . . .'

Cassie said, 'You were human before you were superhuman.'

He coughed once more and fell flat onto his face, dead.

Cassie stood over his body and sighed with deep relief.

Cassie raced back to the hall where Trey still lay. She slid to his side and patted his cheeks.

'Trey! Trey! Can you hear me?'

His eyes fluttered open. 'Is he . . .?'

'Yep. I exploded his lungs under ultra-high pressure.'

Trey nodded. 'Appropriately gruesome death. Nice.'

A sudden groan made them spin.

But it wasn't the Fury. It was Golden Gary, staggering into the hall, limping and clutching his chest.

'You got him?'

'Got him,' Cassie said.

'You always were the smartest of us all,' Gary said with a smile.

'Here.' Cassie pulled out her phone and handed it to Gary. 'We need to get the word out. Can you please connect me to your twelve million followers? That should be enough.'

While Gary did some quick typing on the phone, Cassie

dragged the Fury's corpse into the hall and dumped it onto the floor.

Then she stood beside it as Gary began filming her with the phone.

Cassie looked straight down the lens.

'People of the world, my fellow Americans,' she said. 'You don't know me because for a long time I stayed hidden. Today I couldn't hide anymore. My name is Cassie Cassowitz. I'm the youngest child of Cobalt and I just killed the Fury of Russia. You can call me Cobalt Blue.'

EPILOGUE I

RUSSIAN MILITARY FACILITY SOMEWHERE IN SIBERIA

A concrete-walled laboratory deep beneath a mountain.

A row of six glass tanks lines the walls.

Two Russian men watch the television news as it reports on the death of the Fury of Russia and his sons.

One is a Russian general.

The other is more dangerous.

His round wire-rimmed glasses frame his thin, gaunt face.

He is the final son of the Fury, the Fury of Sevastopol, but he is known in elite Russian military circles simply as the Genius.

'My father should have listened to me. He should have waited. We would have been ready soon.'

On the TV set, he sees the footage of Cassie on Instagram delivering her message to the world.

The Genius watches her closely.

'But it's not a total loss. Now we know about her.'

EPILOGUE II

A LIVING ROOM
SOMEWHERE IN NEVADA

Cobalt Black also watches the footage of Cassie. He smiles, starts clapping at the television.

'Bravo, girl! Bravo. You just opened up a whole new world of possibilities.'

THE END

AN INTERVIEW WITH MATTHEW REILLY

SPOILER WARNING!
The following interview contains SPOILERS from *Cobalt Blue*. Readers who have not yet read the novella are advised to avoid reading this interview as it does give away major plot moments in the book.

After finishing the Jack West series with the epic The One Impossible Labyrinth *last year, you delighted and surprised us all with this superfun superhero book,* Cobalt Blue. *Where did this story come from, and what inspired you to write it as a novella?*

So, *Cobalt Blue* began life as a screenplay. But the thing is, screenplays are much shorter than novels: they're usually around 100 pages of double-spaced text as opposed to 400 pages of single-spaced text in a book. As I wrote the screenplay, I was having so much fun with the world of Cassie, Cobalt, the Fury and the Cobalt superchildren, that I found I wanted to make the story *bigger*. So I reconfigured it as a novella and expanded the world and the characters (in ways that I just couldn't do within the bounds of a screenplay).

The screenplay of *Cobalt Blue* still exists, and its structure is exactly the same as the novella, but it has fewer scenes than the novella. For instance, the cruise liner scene is not in the film script, nor is the action scene at LAX with the Vice President. It also has less character depth than the novella—which is the joy of prose: you can get deeper into the characters.

That said, the script *rocks* and it's a movie I'd very much like to direct at some point!

We are in a golden age of ever-popular superhero films. How do you go about creating a family of superheroes—not to mention a family of supervillains!—and make it feel so fresh and exciting?

It certainly has been a golden period for superhero stories lately. I figure that over the past fifteen years or so, as I've been watching so many excellent superhero movies (Christopher Nolan's Batman trilogy and the Marvel Cinematic Universe), the 'superhero' vibe somehow seeped into me.

The challenge is doing something new. I've watched the superhero TV show, *The Boys*, and while I've enjoyed it, it's a bit too dark for my writing tastes. I still like to experience a story with the 'good guys' as the leads, not the bad guys. To be experiencing a superhero story with Cassie somehow keeps the story hopeful, at least to me.

The key for me with *Cobalt Blue* was giving superheroes to nations and creating a kind of mutually-assured destruction similar to the nuclear stand-off during the Cold War.

Once I did that, the rest of the story almost wrote itself: of course, both countries would try to create offspring from their superpowered heroes; Russia would do that one way, the U.S. would do it another way—and in the middle of all that, Cobalt would have a natural child, too. The superchildren would have different abilities and personalities. Celebrity would follow. And I also found that I could explore the very interesting notion of the superpowered intellects of Cobalt Black and the Fury of Sevastopol. It struck me that a superbrain might drive a person insane. I just found all that very interesting and thus the story was born.

In most superhero stories, the good guys usually survive to fight another day. But in Cobalt Blue, *poor Cassie Cassowitz has a rough day with all the super-siblings that she loses.*

She sure does. I wanted the story to be this grim count-down to a showdown. Cassie watches in horror as the Fury works his way across America toward her, killing her siblings. I like to think that the story has a kind of inexorable momentum to it, a gradually approaching doom. This is why the Fury's murders of the super-siblings are so graphic: I wanted them to be shocking so that Cassie must fear this dreadful ever-approaching villain.

This structure enabled me to insert the nice flashback scenes to convey Cassie's relationships with each of her Cobalt super-siblings, which was also fun.

Cassie is a wonderful new Matthew Reilly hero. While **Cobalt Blue** *is full of big action sequences, Cassie gives us a lot to think about in terms of fame and heroism.*

The title of the novella is the key here, because for me, this story is all about Cassie *choosing* to become Cobalt Blue, as she does in the final line.

As I've grown older, I've found myself more and more fascinated with the concept of 'the hero'. And I've sometimes explored this in the Scarecrow and Jack West novels.

In *Cobalt Blue*, I love the scene where Cassie and Cobalt Black debate being a hero who serves America or one who rules it. Black actually makes some interesting points about choosing to serve versus choosing to rule. We've all been brought up watching Superman choose to defend America, but what if he chose to rule?

Will we see any more of Cobalt Blue in the future?

As the epilogues show, I do have a more ideas for this world and it's a fun world to write in, so I hope so—I just have to find the time!

At the time of this interview you're in Australia, putting the finishing editing touches on your Netflix movie Interceptor, *which will have been released before this book is published. How does it feel now, so close to having your first film (directed by you and co-written with Stuart Beattie) hit screens?*

This is probably a good place to talk about *Interceptor*.

Making *Interceptor* was a blast! As most of my fans know, it has long been my dream to direct an action movie, and with *Interceptor* I finally got that chance. Since I didn't know if I'd get another shot, I just went for it. I literally threw myself into it. I worked solidly on the movie from January 2021 till March 2022 (from pre-production and the shoot to editing and finally to visual effects and sound which stretched into 2022). Directing a movie is a 24/7 experience: you're up at 4:45 a.m. and you work long hours, but I loved it.

The story in *Interceptor* is deceptively simple. The bad guys steal sixteen Russian nuclear missiles and want to fire them on America. But to do that, they first need to disable America's two interceptor bases, one in Alaska, the other in the Pacific Ocean (a converted oil rig called SBX-1—which is real by the way!). Our story begins with the Alaskan facility destroyed. We then go to SBX-1, where we meet our heroine, Captain JJ Collins (played by Elsa Pataky) just as the bad guys who have infiltrated the rig break out their guns and try to take it out. She is determined to defend her interceptor and thus we have our drama. Over the course of the movie, sixteen nukes will be fired at America and she will have to intercept them.

There's so much in *Interceptor*. JJ's history of suffering sexual harassment is inspired by several real-life cases that I read about. I actually wrote the script at the start of 2017 and I wondered if 'sexual harassment in the military' would still be relevant when the movie finally got made. Sadly, it still is. But it's something that I think people should know about, and that's why I included it in the film.

Getting the movie made was a long story, so I'll just provide some of the highlights of that journey. For one thing, one mini-studio in Hollywood loved the script and offered to buy it *as long as I didn't direct* (first-time directors don't have a great reputation in Hollywood, so studios and producers often try to avoid working with them). I insisted that I had to direct. They said it was a dealbreaker. So I walked. And, to their credit, my producers walked with me, hopeful that we would eventually find another home for the movie.

Several actresses passed on the lead role (like the studios, many actors don't want to work with first-time directors either), but then the script found its way to Elsa Pataky and she jumped at it. Turned out, it was exactly the kind of movie she'd been looking for: one with a strong female lead and lots of fun action. Plus, in JJ Collins, I had written a character who would be a role model for Elsa's daughter, which was also something Elsa wanted. Most importantly, Elsa was willing to work with me as the director of the movie!

With Elsa onboard, Netflix quickly joined in and we were off. Looking back, I can honestly say that I now can't see any other actress playing that role. JJ is such a physical character (possessing serious mental toughness, too) and Elsa just *became* her. Elsa got superfit—with Linda Hamilton-level muscles—and she trained and trained and trained for no less than five big fight scenes. And that's not even mentioning her acting skills: put simply, Elsa is a *phenomenal* actress, capable of conveying deep emotions with just the flick of an eye or a sideways glance. And finally, she was just a damned hard worker. She was never *ever* late, she was always prepared and she never complained (even when she was being dunked in cold water on freezing-cold, windy days). She was the consummate professional and all the other cast and crew saw that—and her example permeated their work.

On a thematic level, *Interceptor* is in many ways an allegory for America today. When I started writing it, I wanted the heroine and the villain to simply be from different socioeconomic classes: JJ would be from solid blue-collar stock and Alexander Kessel (played by Luke Bracey) would be from wealth. As I progressed with the writing of the script and added the duplicitous Beaver, I suddenly had an allegory on my hands: a rich aristocrat enlists a redneck and some henchmen to destroy America, which is defended by the honest blue-collar JJ Collins.

As I write this, the movie has not yet been released, so I don't yet know how it will be received. (I'm expecting some anger from some parts of the political spectrum, but you have to expect that; indeed, if you want to make something with an edge, you have to expect that some people will feel strongly about it, both favourably and unfavourably. I mean, look at my Amazon.com review scores: I either get 5 stars or 1 star.)

But in the end, for me the movie is fun and fast and entertaining: a wild ride. Like the books, I just hope people will enjoy it. For those who have read my novels, it is very clearly a 'Matthew Reilly Story': bullet-fast and totally out of control!

Any hints as to what your next novel is about? When can we expect it out?

I'm writing it now. As for when it'll come out, well, it's been a busy few years and I need a rest! I wrote *The One Impossible Labyrinth* within a year of finishing *The Two Lost Mountains* and then I dived straight into directing *Interceptor*, which has been rather all-consuming. (I just happened to have *Cobalt Blue* up my sleeve and it's always nice to release a secret book!). So give me a little time but another novel is on its way.

As always, I just hope you enjoyed the book (and the movie!).

Matthew Reilly
Sydney
March 2022

Keep reading for two Matthew Reilly short stories:

Prequels to
THE JACK WEST JUNIOR NOVELS

and
THE TOURNAMENT

A PREQUEL TO THE
JACK WEST JR NOVELS

MATTHEW REILLY

JACK WEST JR
and the
HERO'S HELMET

Jack West Jr.

Adventurer. Scholar. Warrior.

He is known for his cool head under pressure . . .

. . . and also for the battered fireman's helmet he has worn throughout his adventures.

This is the story of how he got it.

BEWARE OF THE HALF TRUTH.

**YOU MAY HAVE GOTTEN HOLD
OF THE WRONG HALF.**

UNKNOWN

THE TEMPLE OF DENDUR

South of Aswan, Egypt

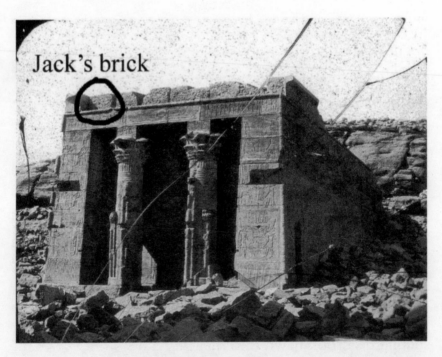

Source: Brooklyn Museum Archives, Goodyear Archival Collection
(via Wikipedia)

1

THE TEMPLE OF DENDUR
8:35 P.M. 24 DECEMBER 1994

Night had fallen by the time Jack West Jr was able to erect his high stepladder and get up close to the roof of the stone temple.

He peered at a single crumbling 2,000-year-old sandstone brick. It was weathered and worn yet oddly beautiful. It was one of eight such bricks that ran along the roofline of the gate of the Egyptian Temple of Dendur.

Peering closer, Jack saw it, and his heart almost skipped a beat.

There, in the top left corner of the brick, was the inscription that he had based his entire thesis upon: a tiny shepherd's crook hewn into the off-yellow stone.

He couldn't believe he was about to do this. If what he had postulated was true, then it would make his name in the world of international archaeology . . . and he was only twenty-five.

He gazed at the stone brick that surmounted the Egyptian temple's entrance and for the hundredth time wondered if there was indeed something embedded *within* that lone brick—

'Mommy! I wanna go *home*!' a child's voice said from somewhere nearby and Jack turned from his perch.

The Sackler Wing of New York's Metropolitan Museum of Art was emptying and the kid who had cried out was one of a dozen or so people remaining in it. The ancient Egyptian Temple of Dendur stood in the middle of the Sackler Wing, a stupendous high-ceilinged glass-walled space that had been purpose-built to house the structure when it had been gifted to the United States by the Egyptian government in 1978.

It had taken thirteen years to dismantle the 800-ton temple—one piece at a time—from its original position on the Nile south of Aswan, ship it to New York, and then re-erect it, once again one piece at a time.

Jack never tired of coming to the Met to see the Temple of Dendur—to see something so monumentally old contained inside something so monumentally modern always gave him a thrill—but apparently that was not the case for this lad.

Jack saw the kid—a sullen-looking boy in NBA everything—and his harried parents. The mother grabbed him by the hand and led him out of the great glass-walled hall.

Jack looked at his watch. It was 8:40 p.m. The Met closed at nine, but they cleared out all the exhibits at 8:45. And when the clock struck 8:45, he would be allowed to do his thing.

Back in those days Jack West Jr was twenty-five and already a decorated member of the SAS. A veteran of the Gulf War—during which he had famously stolen Saddam Hussein's own 747 to escape from Basra—he had sandy blond hair, blue eyes and, at that time, he still had his own left arm. The incident underneath the Kanyamanaga volcano in Africa in which he would lose that arm—and save a newborn baby girl whom he would later name Lily—would not happen for another fifteen months.

But in 1994, having only been recently listed as one of the top ten special forces soldiers in the world, Jack had surprised many when he had abruptly taken a leave of absence from the military. He was going to study ancient history at Trinity College in Dublin under the tutelage of Professor Max T. Epper, the famous Canadian scholar and Jack's good friend.

Jack's main area of interest was Egypt and, with Epper, he had co-authored several articles for scholarly journals about topics as diverse as the location of the lost Mouseion of Alexandria, the true date of the construction of the Sphinx and the capstone that had once stood atop the Great Pyramid of Giza.

But this trip to New York City was something new again.

Jack had come here with Max to find evidence to support his first solo article in the highly esteemed *Journal of Egyptian Archaeology*: after many letters and phone calls, the Met had finally allowed him to come and use a non-invasive technique to see if there was an ancient weapon buried within one of the bricks of the Temple of Dendur.

As the last members of the public ambled out of the Sackler Wing, Jack and Max went about setting up their Ground Penetrating Radar kit at the top of the twenty-foot stepladder.

One of the Met's conditions of their visit—in addition to the absolutely inviolable order that they were not to in any way touch or penetrate the ancient brick—had been that they had to do their work after hours, so as not to impinge upon the general public's viewing time, hence the late hour and the odd date, Christmas Eve.

As Max handed up the last pieces of the GPR kit, Jack caught sight of a figure standing at the back of the hall: a lone man in a tan trench coat with the collar turned up.

Jack frowned. 'Hey, Max. Trench Coat Guy is still here.'

Max Epper turned from his position at the base of the stepladder. 'So he is. Maybe he's as keen on Egypt as we are.'

'Or maybe he's employed by the Met to keep an eye on us,' Jack said. They'd been accompanied by two uniformed security guards ever since they'd arrived earlier that afternoon but this guy had the distinct look of a senior executive who wanted to watch them himself.

'Power please, Max,' Jack said as he lined up the Ground Penetrating Radar sighter at the suspect brick: the second one from the left atop the temple's front-facing roof. The GPR worked by sending a pulse of high-frequency micro-waves into the stone; those waves would then bounce back off any object embedded inside the rock and the pattern they formed would give Jack a clear image of that object.

If it was in there.

'Power is on,' Max called from an outlet by the wall. 'It's now or never. Fire it up.'

'Right,' Jack said. 'Now or never.'

He hit the switch and the GPR fired its pulse into the 2,000-year-old sandstone brick.

The GPR unit pinged and its screen refreshed at ten-second intervals. As it did so, like a naval vessel's radar, the image on it materialised, becoming clearer with every renewal of the screen.

Jack's eyes never left the monitor.

The rectangular outline of the stone brick was depicted in pale grey. Slowly, with each refreshing of the image, a white object began to appear within it.

Jack felt his heart begin to race as the image resolved into something resembling a 't'.

'Come on, baby . . .' Jack breathed.

His postulation in his article was that there was a knife in the brick, a knife that had belonged to Osiris, the famed Egyptian god of the afterlife, the underworld and resurrection. Of course, Jack didn't think Osiris had been a god at all: his theory was that Osiris had been a famous warrior or king, just one whose great deeds during his life had been elevated to god-like status over the millennia.

As the image resolved further, Jack began to smile. The 't' was looking more and more like the hilt and cross-guard of a knife.

'Max!' he called. 'Get ready to be happy. I think we got it . . .'

At which moment, all the lights in the Metropolitan Museum of Art suddenly went out, the Sackler Wing was plunged into darkness and an emergency siren began to blare in Jack's ears.

2

Jack spun from his position atop the stepladder and immediately he smelled it. Smoke.

He couldn't tell where it was coming from, but it was definitely in the air. 'This is not happening,' he said. He looked around the vast darkened hall, suspicious at the timing of the interruption.

No, it's just a bad coincidence.

A way-too-pleasant automated woman's voice came in over the loudspeakers: 'Ladies and gentlemen, this is an evacuation. Please proceed calmly to the nearest exit. We apologise for this inconvenience. Your cooperation is appreciated.'

Jack reluctantly descended the stepladder, rejoining Max and the two security guards at its base.

As they headed for the exit, Jack saw Trench Coat Guy also turning to go.

Jack, Max and the security guards wended their way through the splendid corridors of the Metropolitan Museum of Art, joining the moving crowd of people heading for the front entrance: the last remaining visitors to the museum and a handful of staff members who had still been in the building.

Sirens could be heard outside.

As Jack and Max came to the front entrance of the Met and headed out, a gaggle of five firefighters with helmets that read fdny precinct 17 shoved past them, rushing inside, leaving a red fire engine, also labelled '17', parked on the kerb of Fifth Avenue at the base of the Met's high entry steps, its flashing emergency lights bathing the area in a strobing red glow.

Jack sighed.

It was cold out here. A light snow fell on Fifth Avenue. More Fire Department of New York trucks arrived.

'Who would believe it?' Jack said to Max. 'Just as I saw the knife . . .'

After a few minutes, the five firefighters emerged, their commander holding up his hands. 'It's okay, folks. Just a broken fuse that set off the smoke detectors. It's all good now.'

The five firemen hurried away, climbing back into the truck marked '17'. Max and the security guards turned to head back inside.

At that moment, a small boy standing near Jack said to his father, 'That's not right.'

'What's not right, son?' the boy's dad said.

'Truck 17 is a ladder truck, not a regular engine,' the boy said.

Jack frowned. 'Excuse me, kid, but what did you say?'

'I love firetrucks,' the boy said earnestly. 'Every fireman has the number of his truck on his helmet. If his helmet says "17", then he's from truck number 17. FDNY truck 17 is famous; it's a ladder truck. But that one over there'—he pointed to the engine marked '17'—'is just a regular fire engine. It's got the wrong number on it.'

Jack gazed at the No. 17 fire engine as it began to pull away from the kerb.

As he was doing this, the commander of one of the *other* firetrucks ascended the stairs and called out as if he were the most senior man there: 'Okay, what's going on here?'

Jack turned to Max. 'Max, quick, go back inside now. Check the temple. Keep your cell phone on.'

'What about you?' Max asked.

Jack was already stepping slowly towards the fire engine marked '17'. 'I'll be here, watching *them* . . .'

Professor Max Epper knew that tone of voice, so he knew not to argue.

He hurried back inside the museum, with the two guards. Max was also younger then, faster, too. Within a minute, he burst back into the Sackler Wing and beheld the Temple of Dendur in its glorious exhibition space.

He saw it right away.

Saw the roof of the temple.

The second brick from the left—the brick Jack had been analysing—*had been vandalised, smashed open*: the top half of the oblong stone was now simply gone, crudely hacked away with a pickaxe or something similar . . . like a fireman's axe.

Max spoke into his phone. 'Jack, your brick's been smashed open. Whatever you found inside it, someone just took it!'

Outside, on the front steps of the Metropolitan Museum of Art, Jack held his phone to his ear, walking slowly toward the fire engine marked '17'.

At Max's words, his eyes snapped up to the truck's cab and locked onto the 'commander' of the firetruck and in that instant their eyes met and they both knew exactly what the other was thinking. The commander of the fake firetruck yelled to his driver, 'Go! Go!'

The truck squealed out from the kerb, wheels spinning on the snow-slicked road.

And Jack West started running after it.

3

It was the brief wheel-spin in the snow that allowed Jack to catch it.

That ever-so-brief skid on the spot allowed Jack to cover the last ten yards and dive full-length for the tail-gate of the escaping fire engine.

His fingers caught the truck's rear bumper just as the big red truck peeled away from the front entrance of the Met—lights blazing, sirens wailing—and started speeding south down Fifth Avenue.

Jack's feet bounced on the icy road as he was dragged along behind the accelerating firetruck.

A cluster of metal hose valves and switches were mounted above him, plus a thin seven-foot access ladder attached to the rear flank of the fire engine; it led up to the roof of the truck and all the various hoses and fire-fighting paraphernalia up there.

Jack reached for the little access ladder, clutched hold of it and began climbing.

With its lights flashing and sirens blaring, the truck zoomed down Fifth, the already sparse Christmas Eve traffic parting before it like the Red Sea before Moses. Only a few of the drivers who pulled over to let it pass glimpsed the tiny figure climbing up the little ladder on the tailgate of the furiously speeding firetruck.

Jack reached the top of the ladder and beheld the roof of the fire engine, just as a man dressed in a firefighter's outfit came rushing at him, face twisted in anger, fists flying.

For this man was no New York City firefighter: he was an imposter dressed as one.

Jack grappled with the imposter in the flashing red glare of the fire engine's lights, wrestling desperately from his inferior position at the very edge of the roof, trying not to get thrown off the back of the speeding firetruck.

One thing was instantly clear: his opponent could fight. Jack had been an elite soldier and this guy clearly had similar training.

Suddenly, his assailant threw a punch but Jack caught the man's fist, and in a fleeting instant, Jack saw a tattoo on the man's wrist.

A tattoo of a fish with a crucifix inside it.

Jack's mind whirled. He knew that symbol, but seeing it on this man's wrist, in the middle of a desperate fight, didn't make sense.

It was the mark of Opus Dei, the notoriously secretive, ultra-conservative cabal within the Catholic Church. *But what did Opus Dei or the Catholic Church have to do with ancient Egyptian temples?*[1]

The next moment, Jack's attacker head-butted him with the leading edge of his FDNY helmet . . . or at least he tried to.

Jack dodged the blow at the last second and said, 'That's dirty pool, asshole. Can't let you do that again.'

So Jack reached out and snatched at the man's helmet at the same time as the man drew a gun from his waistband.

Jack saw the gun and his eyes went wide, and on a reflex he shifted his weight and grabbed something next to him as he yanked on the chin-strap of his attacker's helmet and threw them both backwards . . . *off the rear of the speeding firetruck and onto Fifth Avenue!*

Jack's attacker hit the road hard—helmetless—and tumbled away down Fifth Avenue, receding quickly behind the truck.

But Jack didn't.

The object he'd grabbed from the roof of the fire engine was one of its firehoses, which meant that when he hit the roadway, the firehose went taut and like a whip snapping, it dragged Jack along behind the speeding firetruck. It

---

1 This was many years before Jack discovered that the modern Catholic Church—with its many references to sun-worship—was the contemporary incarnation of an ancient Egyptian sun-cult known as the Cult of Amon-Ra. See: Seven Ancient Wonders.

was only the snow-slicked road that stopped Jack from being seriously grazed by the experience.

Strangely, by virtue of the way he'd grabbed his attacker's chin-strap, Jack now gripped the firehose with the strap of the man's fake 'FDNY 17' helmet wedged between his fingers and the firehose. He didn't dare let go of the hose, so the helmet was coming with him.

A few seconds later, the firetruck's lights and sirens suddenly went quiet and the fire engine swung left off Fifth Avenue, sending Jack rolling onward down Fifth.

When he finally rolled to a stop he scrambled off the snow-covered road, diving onto the sidewalk to narrowly avoid being hit by a couple of honking taxi cabs. Lying on his belly on the icy sidewalk, Jack saw the fake fire engine parked down a side street—50th Street—its fake firemen scrambling out of it and disappearing into an alleyway behind the old dark building that adjoined 50th and fronted onto Fifth Avenue.

One of the 'firemen', Jack saw, carried a piece of the brick from the Temple of Dendur under his arm.

Jack's eyes rose, taking in the grim dark building they'd scurried behind.

It had two horn-like belltowers and its brooding Neo-Gothic entrance stood in stark contrast to the more modern glass and steel buildings of New York around it.

It was St Patrick's Cathedral.

The pre-eminent Catholic Church in New York City and seat of the Cardinal of New York, one of the four most powerful Catholic clergymen in America.

Gasping for breath, Jack dragged himself off the ground and ran for the alleyway after the fleeing 'firemen'.

The moment he turned the corner of the alleyway, he froze. What he saw shocked him.

He saw a lone man standing amid the five fake firemen. The man had already shot dead four of them—they lay on the ground, in icy puddles of melted snow with holes in their foreheads—and now the lone man stood, bathed in shadow, with a silenced pistol levelled at the head of the leader of the group.

Jack ducked behind a dumpster and watched fearfully as the lone man took the piece of sandstone from the fake fireman.

Even from this distance, from behind the dumpster, Jack could see the handle of the ancient knife embedded in the broken-open sandstone brick.

The Knife of Osiris.

And then, making Jack jump, the lone man spoke to the commander of the fake fire team. 'This is not yours to take. It belongs to my master. It is not yet time to use the keyblade.'

The gunshot that followed barely made a sound.

The back of the fake fireman's head blew out, spraying

blood, and he collapsed like a puppet whose strings had been cut.

Then, holding the broken brick from the Temple of Dendur in one hand and the silenced pistol in the other, the lone man turned to go. As he passed through a beam of light, Jack saw his face and recognised him.

It was Trench Coat Guy, the man who had been silently watching Jack and Max all afternoon in the Sackler Wing.

Jack ducked away from the alleyway, crossing Fifth Avenue and taking cover inside a liquor store so as not to be seen by the man.

He watched from afar as the man in the trench coat emerged from the side street flanking the cathedral, carrying the ancient brick under his coat.

Jack watched him. There was something about him—about the way he carried himself, a kind of eerie self-possession—that Jack had seen in only one kind of person before: *assassins*.

Jack West was many things—a great soldier, a good fighter and a fair historian—but without serious weaponry, there was no way he could get the better of this guy tonight.

The man in the trench coat looked both ways before he hailed a cab and disappeared into the New York night.

Jack could only watch him go.

He stepped out onto the sidewalk of Fifth Avenue, peering down the long wide boulevard on that cold winter's night, before suddenly he looked down at his own right hand.

Still gripped tightly in it—indeed, Jack had forgotten he was even holding it—was his only memento of what would remain one of the most bizarre evenings of his life: the helmet of the fake fireman he had fought on the back of the firetruck, a helmet marked fdny precinct 17.

Jack would never forget the Knife of Osiris or the strange word the assassin had used to describe it: keyblade. He would also wear that helmet for many years, using it to ward off falling rocks and troublesome waterflows in booby-trapped places all around the world . . . and also as a constant reminder to himself that not everyone is always who they seem.

THE TEMPLE OF DENDUR

(as it appears today in the Metropolitan Museum of Art,
New York City, U.S.A.)

THE END

A PREQUEL TO
THE TOURNAMENT

MATTHEW REILLY

ROGER ASCHAM
and the
KING'S LOST GIRL

It is costly wisdom that is bought by experience.

– ROGER ASCHAM

CAMBRIDGE
FEBRUARY, 1546

**Seven months before the events
depicted in *The Tournament***

1

KING'S COLLEGE, CAMBRIDGE
FEBRUARY 1546

It was always a celebrated occasion when the king came to visit Cambridge . . . for everyone except Roger Ascham.

The chapel at King's College, stupendous and imposing at the best of times, had been converted into a colossal audience chamber for King Henry and it was filled to bursting point with academics, students, puffed-up local nobles and the awestruck townsfolk of Cambridge.

The king sat on a high throne that had been placed on a stage at the front of the chapel's three-hundred-foot-long nave, which was only right, as just two years previously he had paid for the completion of the chapel, in doing so finishing a building project that had been begun almost one hundred years earlier at the command of Henry VI.

Outside, a steady snow fell. It had been a cold and bitter winter. The trees, roads and lawns of Cambridge were covered in white and the river had frozen over.

From his throne, Henry attended to the business of being king—honouring the local noblemen, gifting money, hearing petitions; he even thanked the Earl of Cumberland's bastard son, a student at the College, for the repair and reconstruction work the young man had carried out on the ruins of Cambridge Castle.

Corpulent yet still commanding, with his heavy bearded jowls and deep voice, the king was by turns charming and frightening. He may have needed wheeled machines to move up and down stairways but he knew how to hold court and he had this one in the palm of his hand.

As the business of the king's visit was taking place at the front of the great space, sitting quietly at the back, unnoticed by all, were two figures: Roger Ascham and his young royal student.

Ascham sighed inwardly. He knew what was coming. He had endured it before. Still, it was always unnerving to be commanded to report to a king who had renounced the Catholic Church, dissolved its monasteries and ordered the execution of two of his six wives.

Ascham wondered who had complained to the king this time. He guessed it had been Primrose Ponsonby—who had complained to the king about Ascham's teaching methods on six previous occasions—but it could have been any of a dozen people.

Roger Ascham was thirty years old and a highly regarded professor of Latin and Greek at Cambridge. He was of modest build and he had a thick mop of brown hair that covered his oversized ears. But his eyes were sharp, they took in everything. In addition to his duties at Cambridge he had recently taken on the role of overseeing the education of the third in line to the English throne.

That individual happened to be the twelve-year-old girl sitting quietly by his side—her head bent reading a book, her feet swinging happily, unable to reach the floor—a delightful young lady known to Ascham as Bess but to everyone at court at Elizabeth. Her usually wild curly red hair had been tightly braided for this unexpected visit from her father. Right now, despite the murmuring, movement and general excitement in the great room around her, she was totally absorbed in her book: a history of Cleopatra that Ascham himself had recently translated.

While he waited to be raked over the coals by the famously intemperate king—and he and Bess had been waiting all morning; it looked like Henry had chosen to see them last of all—Ascham examined a most unusual object in his hands: a brass mariner's quadrant that he had been tinkering with. The quadrant had long been used for celestial navigation at sea, but Ascham was frustrated with its limitations on a rolling ship's deck, so he had attached a couple of mirrors to the device, plus a sighting tube, which he hoped would make it work better—

'Excuse me, good sir, but is that a quadrant you have there?' The voice was cultured, firm, confident.

Ascham looked up.

A young man in his twenties stood before him, a student. A student, Ascham realised, that he knew.

The lad's name was Timothy Higginbotham but the plainness of his name had not stopped the rumour-mongers at Cambridge—they could smell anyone with blood ties to a title from ten miles away—from figuring out very quickly who he really was: Timothy Higginbotham was the bastard son of the Earl of Cumberland. And he was clearly a beloved son: despite his illegitimacy, the Earl had sent him to Cambridge with a sizeable pension.

Ascham handed the young man the quadrant. 'Yes, it is but with some modifications of my own design.'

Higginbotham took the device and turned it sideways to look at it more closely.

'I love to know the inner workings of things,' he said absently. 'I like your modifications. They would compensate for the rocking of a ship, allowing you to sight your star and the horizon with greater ease.'

Ascham was both surprised and impressed at the speed with which the young man had assessed the purpose of his adjustments.

'Why, thank you. You are Cumberland's boy, are you not? The one who has been repairing the old castle?'

'I am.'

'I confess I do not venture to that part of town very often so I have not seen your work at the ruins. You are a student here? What are you studying?'

'Medicine,' the lad answered without looking up, still gazing at the quadrant. 'I want to be a surgeon.'

Ascham nodded. 'Good for you. That is a fine calling—'

'*MR ROGER ASCHAM AND HER HIGHNESS, THE PRINCESS ELIZABETH!*' the King's herald's voice boomed above the din.

Ascham retrieved his quadrant from the lad and, taking Bess's hand in his, strode down the length of the hall.

The crowd parted like the Red Sea before Moses as Ascham and Bess made their way toward the throne. Ascham caught many a curious glance and even a few pitying ones from members of the throng as he passed them by.

And there, looming at the end of the pathway made by the crowd, sat King Henry VIII, legs spread wide, fists resting on his armrests, staring down at them. Ascham wondered if anyone else saw the irony of a king who had dispossessed the Catholic Church of its riches sitting on a throne in a grand chapel that had been built for that very Church. He doubted it.

Ascham and Bess stopped before the king, holding hands, and for a horrifying moment the hall went silent. The king's frown was even more severe than usual.

And then his face broke into a broad grin. 'Come here, my gorgeous little princess!'

Bess walked toward her father, shoulders hunched and head bent, blushing.

In so many ways, Ascham thought, she was beyond her years—but in the presence of her father she became a little girl again. So confident and assured in private, now she moved with the stilted awkwardness of every twelve-year-old girl. Ascham's heart went out to her.

The king took her hand gently in his and suddenly became the doting parent. 'Are you doing your sums, little one?'

'Yes, Father.'

'And your Greek? I am told it is improving.'

'Oh, it is, Father. Mr Ascham is frightfully good at the ancient languages.'

At the mention of Ascham's name, Henry cast a glance at him. 'And how is your chess, Elizabeth? Have you beaten your teacher yet?'

'No,' Bess said sadly. 'He continues to get the better of me. But I am improving, Father, and I shall beat him one day. I am determined to.'

Ascham offered the king an apologetic half-smile. His crushing victories over Bess at chess had been the subject of their last meeting.

Henry kept his eyes on Ascham as he spoke. 'If your teacher is equipping you with determination, then I approve of those lessons. It is a worthy virtue to possess. Now, run along, my sweetling, I have matters to discuss with your schoolmaster. Master Rusting, please take my delightful daughter to the kitchen and find her something sweet and tasty.'

Bess was whisked away by the king's usher.

No sooner was she out of the room than the king rounded on Ascham.

'Ascham, what in fucking hell were you fucking thinking when you took my fucking daughter to a fucking slaughterhouse last month?'

Ascham stood his ground. So that was it.

'Your Majesty, I merely wished for Bess to learn where her food comes from,' he replied evenly. 'Every common farmer's child knows how a leg of beef arrives at their table, but Bess did not. I felt that a potential future Queen of England—'

The crowd tittered. Elizabeth was third in line to the throne and if her half-brother ascended to that throne, married and had children, she would be shunted further down the line of succession. Her chances of becoming queen were wildly remote and the whole room knew it.

Ascham went on, heedless of their mocking. '—I felt that a potential future Queen of England should know this.'

Henry stared at Ascham for a long moment, not speaking.

The hall fell silent again.

Then the king spat, 'Hell and fucking damnation, Ascham. Just don't do it again. I'm sick of getting fucking complaints about your fucking teaching methods. That is all. Now, clear this hall!'

The king's guards began herding the crowd out of the vast chapel. His humiliation over, Ascham was making to leave as well when the king called, 'Not you, Ascham! You will stay!'

And that was a something Roger Ascham had not expected.

Moments later, the great hall was empty, save for Ascham, the king and the king's chief aide, Sir Harold Rigby.

'Ascham,' the king said in a very different tone. 'A most . . . unusual . . . matter has arisen and I require your assistance.'

'My assistance, Your Majesty?' Ascham did not know where this was going.

'When I come to Cambridge, I enjoy the, ah, ministrations of a young lady at Napier's establishment, an Italian girl by the named of Isabella. She is a most beautiful thing and she has talents that I have found in no other lady in England.'

Ascham said nothing. The king's visits to Napier's brothel while in Cambridge were well known.

The king went on: 'You will, therefore, understand the frustration I felt when I arrived here this week to discover that the girl is not at Napier's.'

'She no longer works as a prostitute?' Ascham asked.

'No,' Sir Harold Rigby interjected. 'The girl is missing and your king would like her found.'

2

Ascham blinked.

'Your Majesty, I am flattered to be asked to find this girl for you, but I am at a loss. Surely you have a half-dozen men better suited to this task than I. Men more at home visiting dens of, ahem, pleasure, or trackers or hunters, like Sir Roderick of York. He is an unmatched hunter, surely he would be a fine tracker of a missing girl.'

Henry stared directly at Ascham. 'I dispatched Sir Roderick three days ago on exactly this mission. Come with me.'

Henry and Rigby led Ascham to a small stable behind the great chapel. Snowflakes drifted down all around them. Mounds of snow lay heaped against the stable's outer wall. Henry pushed open its doors and Ascham beheld a man's body lying inside a stall.

Henry said, 'As I said, I dispatched Sir Roderick on this mission three days ago. His body was found lying face-down in the snow in the woods near Vicar's Brook on the south side of town this morning.'

Ascham stared at the corpse, swallowing hard. Sir Roderick had been a big man, powerful, a warrior's warrior. Now his body lay in the freezing horse stall like a pale slab of meat.

Henry stepped up beside Ascham, also gazing at the body of the hunter.

'Roderick was a fine knight and an exceptional huntsman. It is hard to imagine any man getting the better of him,' the king said. 'Whoever killed him is formidable, Mr Ascham. My favourite girl is missing and my best man, sent in pursuit of her, is dead. *I want to know what is going on.* You're a most peculiar fellow, Ascham, I won't deny it, but there is always a logic to your madness, a shrewd logic that I do not see often, which is why I tolerate your occasionally bizarre lessons with my sweet Elizabeth. You think outside the usual. You see beyond the normal. This situation is beyond the normal. I want my girl found and I want to know who took her so that I may torture him myself before I cut off his fucking head and mount it on a fucking stake.'

Henry turned to Ascham. 'Can you do this for me?'

'I will do my very best, Your Majesty.'

'Rigby will give you whatever assistance you need. *Find her*, Mr Ascham.'

The king left. Ascham did not.

He turned to Rigby. 'Let's take this body to the school of medicine. I wish to examine it.'

*

An hour later, the body of Sir Roderick lay on a wooden bench surrounded by the gruesome tools of the surgical trade. The skin on his face was completely white from the cold, Ascham noted, white as a ghost.

Alongside Ascham was his friend and head of the school of medicine, John Blyth.

'All right, Roger,' Blyth said after Ascham had briefed him on the identity of the dead man and the manner of the discovery of his body. 'What do you want to know?'

'I want to know how he died.'

Blyth snorted. 'If he is one of the king's men, he probably drank too much wine, collapsed in the snow and froze to death.'

'Indulge me,' Ascham said.

As Blyth began sorting his instruments, Ascham set about removing the dead man's boots.

He paused.

There were curious clumps of yellow-flecked dirt wedged in the soles of Sir Roderick's boots.

'John, do you know what this yellow dirt is?' he asked. 'It looks like a variety of sulphur deposit.'

Blyth glanced over at it. 'There are several sulphurous springs in these parts. Make an ungodly smell, they do.'

'While I do enjoy the odd walk,' Ascham said, 'I do not

wander as far in my ambulations as you do, John. Where are these springs? Are they on the south side of town near Vicar's Brook, perhaps?'

'No, there are none there,' Blyth said. 'There are perhaps a dozen of them but they are mainly to the north and west of Cambridge.'

Blyth commenced his examination of the corpse and after about an hour he reported to Ascham: 'Perhaps I should show more pause before I disparage the king's associates. Your man here didn't freeze to death at all. He drowned. His lungs are filled with water. He was dead well before his body froze.'

'He drowned *then* froze?' asked Ascham.

Blyth said, 'Yes. But then . . . no, that's just ridiculous.'

'Tell me anyway,' Ascham said.

'Well, you said his body was discovered lying face-down in the snow near Vicar's Brook. If he drowned, wouldn't he be found *in* the very lake or river in which he drowned, or at least on the shore of it? Drowned men do not stagger out onto land. This man drowned and was then *taken* from whatever body of water in which he drowned and placed on land, in snow, to make us think he froze to death.'

Ascham stared at the body, thinking.

'How very peculiar. Thank you for your help, John. I shall ensure that the king hears of it. I, however, have more inquiries to make, the first of which is to visit our missing girl's place of employment.'

3

Thirty minutes later, Roger Ascham strode down the main street of Cambridge, coat wrapped tightly around his body, braced against the driving snow. It was getting late in the afternoon and few people were out in the ghastly weather.

He had left Bess in the care of his good friend Gilbert Giles, with instructions that Giles give her a lesson in secular philosophy. Ascham knew full well that neither Giles nor Bess would follow his instructions. Instead, while he ventured out into the terrible weather, they would almost certainly sit by the fire and play chess—Giles was the best player at Cambridge and Elizabeth, frustrated at losing constantly to Ascham, would no doubt ask Giles for some winning strategies.

Ascham arrived at his destination and scowled: Napier's brothel. With a sigh, he entered the house of ill repute.

It was warm inside the brothel, thanks to a blazing fire in a corner of the ante-room. The entry area was large, with lush rugs and expensive velvet curtains. Six young women with painted faces and wearing only their undergarments sauntered around the room. Business was clearly good at Napier's.

Ascham was greeted by a young woman with curly orange hair and wearing just a petticoat. Her name was Georgiana.

When Ascham asked to speak with the owner, Mr Napier, Georgiana fetched him and Ascham was surprised to be met by a short, fresh-faced and beardless man barely twenty years of age.

'Mr Napier? I am Roger Ascham, here at the command of His Majesty, King Henry. I have been commissioned by the king to inquire into the whereabouts of an Italian girl named Isabella who is said to work at this establishment. You are the owner of this house, are you not?'

The young man nodded. 'I am.'

'Forgive me, but you strike me as rather young to be the owner of such a large establishment.'

'It was my father's. I have only just inherited it. My father . . . died . . . recently.'

There was something in the way he said it that caught Ascham short.

'How recently?' he asked.

'Ten days ago.'

'Forgive me for asking,' Ascham pressed, 'but may I inquire *how* he died?'

Young Napier pursed his lips and threw a glance at Georgiana nearby. 'Let us not discuss it in here.' He grabbed a thick fur-lined coat. 'Come outside.'

Moments later, Ascham found himself standing out in the cold with Napier.

'My father was murdered,' Napier said flatly. 'He was found with his head removed from his body over on the eastern side of town.'

'His head had been *cut off*?' Ascham asked.

'Cleanly,' Napier said. 'Without a nick or a shred to the surrounding skin. A shepherd found his body near the sheep track over by the Mill Cemetery. He found the corpse lying in the snow with the head just sitting there beside it. My father had gone in search of the very girl you seek: Isabella.'

Ascham felt his throat tighten.

He did not mention to Napier the fate of Sir Roderick. Isabella, it seemed, was a dangerous girl. Those who went in search of her met untimely and unpleasant ends and now he himself bore that task.

Napier went on: 'Isabella was a particularly lovely girl, spritely and vivacious, with flowing dark hair, enormous brown eyes and a beautiful smile. She was also, I must say, very skilled at the erotic arts. As you are clearly aware, she was a special favourite of the king's when he came to Cambridge to visit.'

'Do you know anything of the girl's final movements?' Ascham asked. 'For instance, who her last customer was?'

'For the sake of discretion, we do not keep written records of our customers and our girls,' Napier said. 'But our memories are good, my father's in particular.'

'You think he went in search of her final customer?' Ascham asked.

'Yes. Occasionally, for our richer customers or those gentlemen who do not wish to be seen on our premises, we send our girls to their residences. Isabella's last job, I am told, was at a customer's residence and my father, it seems, went to that residence to find her.'

'And he did not return.'

'And he did not return,' Napier agreed.

Ascham frowned. 'Tell me again, where was your father's body found?'

Napier turned and pointed. 'At the edge of the Mill Cemetery, about a mile that way.'

As the young man raised his arm to point eastward, Ascham saw something trickle off his back and fall to the snowy ground: some grains of yellow soil, sulphur-like dirt of the kind he had seen on the boots of Sir Roderick. The sandy substance had dropped out of the thick fur lining that covered Napier's neck and shoulders

A chill ran through Ascham. Could this diminutive man have been the one who had killed Sir Roderick? It didn't seem likely but then—

'Mr Napier,' he said, trying to keep his voice even, 'your coat, may I ask how you acquired it?'

'This?' Napier looked down at it. 'Why, it was my father's. It was a gift from the king himself, as thanks for bringing the girl Isabella to his attention a few years ago. As you can see, it is of exceptional quality.'

Ascham's eyes narrowed. 'It was your father's . . .' His mind was turning now. 'Wait, was your father *wearing* this coat when his body was found near the cemetery?'

'Yes, he was.'

'When his head was severed, his body fell into the yellow-flecked dirt . . .' Ascham said, thinking aloud. '*Napier and Roderick were killed in the same place*. And yet they were found far apart, at the southern and eastern extremities of Cambridge.'

'Roderick?' Napier said, perplexed. 'The southern and eastern extremities? I'm sorry, but what the Devil are you talking about?'

Ascham snapped back to attention. 'My apologies, young sir. My mind was running away with things. There is more to this than just the death of your father. Thank you, you have been very helpful indeed.'

4

Their meeting over, Napier went back inside his establishment. Ascham turned and began walking up the snow-covered street.

He thought about the yellow soil. According to Blyth, it could be found around springs in any of a dozen places to the north and west of the wider Cambridge area, but which place specifically?

Lost in thought, Ascham had not gone a hundred paces when a woman's voice stopped him. 'Good sir?'

He turned to find the young red-haired woman from Napier's standing before him in a hooded cloak, the girl named Georgiana.

'Forgive me, sir,' she said, 'but I could not help overhearing earlier when you told Mr Napier that you were inquiring into the whereabouts of Isabella. She was my good friend and I am desperately aggrieved by her disappearance. The other girls are also fearful for word has spread among the ladies of our profession in these parts.'

'What do you mean?' Ascham asked.

Georgiana looked about herself anxiously. 'Lewd women are disappearing. Three from Peterborough, all from different houses, two from Bedford, again both from different establishments, and three also from Colchester, again all from separate brothels. No-one has made this connection except for us lewd women and the sheriffs and noblemen do not care for our opinions or fears.'

Ascham frowned in thought. The towns of Peterborough, Bedford and Colchester formed a wide circle around Cambridge.

'I care for what you say,' he said. 'So our abductor is not only dangerous, he is also shrewd. He targets prostitutes, probably because they are often itinerant or foreign-born and so have few relatives or friends in a town. They are not missed. And he is careful to take only *one* woman from each house of ill repute—and then from different towns—so few notice . . . few, that is, except women in your trade.'

'Yes, sir. That's absolutely right,' Georgiana said. 'Many of us girls are very afraid, sir. Some of us are planning to leave this town, leave the whole area, to get as far away as we can from the monster stealing women in our trade.'

At her words, Ascham's head snapped up.

'To get as far away as you can . . .' he repeated. He looked about himself, thinking. He needed a—

He turned to face the girl. 'Young lady, thank you for the information you have given me. It may be more important than you can imagine. I fear I must away now. I need to find a map.'

Ascham found a map of Cambridge in King's College and took it to John Blyth's rooms.

He unrolled the map, spread it out over a desk and examined it. 'Sir Roderick's body was found here, by Vicar's Brook, on the south side of town,' he said to Blyth as he placed a stone on a spot on the southern quarter of the map.

'And Napier's body, headless, was found by the Mill Cemetery, to the east of the town centre, here.' He placed another stone on the map.

'What are you thinking, Roger?' Blyth asked.

'I am thinking,' Ascham said, 'that our killer is trying to throw any would-be investigator off the scent by depositing the bodies *as far away as he can* from the site of their deaths. So I must find a location in Cambridge which possesses this peculiar yellow soil but which is also as far from these two places as possible.'

'*Here*,' Blyth said, planting his index finger on a point in the north-western corner of the map. 'There is a sizeable deposit of sulphurous dirt here, by a spring that was converted into a moat.'

Ascham peered at the map. The spot Blyth was indicating was almost exactly equidistant from the two locations marked with stones, as far from them as possible.

There was one other thing about the location Blyth had indicated.

His finger had fallen on an icon on the map marked: 'CAMBRIDGE CASTLE'.

5

It was getting dark when Roger Ascham stepped off the main northern road onto the yellow-flecked dirt of a trail that led through dense forest to the ruins of Cambridge Castle.

Built many centuries before, the castle had long ago fallen into disrepair, its stonework cannibalised to build the university's colleges.

There was precious little left of the main building anymore. However, its ancient dungeon still stood, a three-storey structure nestled in the middle of a pond with only a low bridge giving access to it. Up until the last century, this dungeon, with ghastly machines of torture still lining its walls, had been used as something of a local gaol till it, too, fell into disuse.

The forest around the castle had encroached across the trail and in the dimming light of the afternoon and the ever-falling snow, Ascham wondered if he should wait until morning to investigate the ruins: if he took too long or lost his way, finding his way back in darkness could prove difficult, even deadly, given the cold.

But he calculated that he had enough time to make it there and back and so he pressed on, pushing aside branches and vines as he trod down the dirt path.

Many of the branches framing the path had been cut back and Ascham recalled that the Earl of Cumberland's bastard son had been undertaking some reconstruction work on the old castle's dungeon. Due to his duties overseeing the education of Princess Elizabeth, Ascham had been spending less time in Cambridge of late, so he was only dimly aware of these repairs.

He ventured deeper into the forest, turned a corner and suddenly found himself facing the dungeon. Rising out of the middle of a moat, veiled in the slow-falling snow, with its hardy stonework and tiny barred windows, it looked like something from another, harsher time.

The pond around it was completely frozen over, the only access to the dungeon a low wooden bridge with no handrails, just thick beams on either side.

The view of the dungeon had seized Ascham's attention and it was precisely then that he felt an ever-so-gentle tug on his ankle and out of the corner of his eye, he saw something move. On instinct he ducked and—*whoosh!*—something swung down out of the branches above his head and swept by at the exact height where his neck had been.

The whooshing noise was quickly followed by a thud and Ascham looked up from his crouched position to see a scythe-blade—hanging from an ingenious metal swing—lodged in a branch above and behind him.

He had, of course, tripped a length of twine—artfully disguised as a stray vine—causing the swingblade to be released from a perch above him and rush at his neck.

A booby trap.

Ascham swallowed.

It was the same fiendish mechanism, no doubt, that had severed Napier senior's head. Ascham looked at the ground and saw that the path here contained large swathes of the yellow-flecked soil he had already seen twice that day.

Ascham's heart began to pound. He was actually a little surprised at himself.

He had found the lair of the killer.

But he was no huntsman or sword-wielding knight. He wasn't even carrying his beloved bow today, having not thought he would need it when he had appeared before the king that morning. Goodness, he was just a teacher!

Napier had come here, because he knew where he had sent the Italian girl . . . and he had come to a grisly end.

And so had Sir Roderick—how he had found the place, Ascham didn't know, but he guessed it had to do with his hunter's mind. Whatever had led him here, Ascham was keenly aware of what had happened to Sir Roderick once he'd got here. A far more physically powerful man than Ascham, he had come to this place and not emerged alive.

Ascham resolved to race back to King's College to inform the king and return with armed escorts.

But first he had to do one thing: since he didn't want the killer who lurked here to know anyone had come this way, he reset the swingblade that had almost decapitated him, replacing its trip-rope as well.

Ascham had only just set it back in place and was turning to leave when he heard a terrifying sound.

A woman's scream.

It had come from the dungeon.

A desperate shriek of terror.

'Someone's alive in there . . .' Ascham said aloud as he broke into a run and dashed toward the grim dungeon.

He came to the low wooden bridge spanning the frozen pond and hurried across it, his feet pounding on its slats.

Then he entered the dungeon and his breath caught in his throat.

6

What Ascham beheld in that dungeon was the stuff of nightmares. He recoiled in revulsion.

From an elevated platform he saw an old stone-walled chamber lit by flaming torches and filled with awful machines of torture: body-sized sarcophagi fitted with spikes, hanging cages suspended above hot coals or icy baths, iron helmets with no eyeholes, a pillory, two racks and . . .

. . . *Good God*, Ascham thought . . .

. . . and every single one of the hideous contraptions had a young woman imprisoned inside it or manacled to it.

The two women on the racks were dead. Their innards lay exposed, cut open, not in a butcher-like manner but in a more exact, precise way.

Ascham did a quick tally: there were eight women in total, all for the most part undressed. Some groaned, one sobbed, another whimpered while yet another screamed from her cage above the icy bath—a scream that none would hear, save for Ascham, for they were several miles from any kind of habitation.

'For heaven's sake, do something, man.' Ascham said to himself, snapping out of the horrified trance into which he had fallen.

The depraved villain responsible for this hellish scene was apparently not in residence, so Ascham leapt into action, dashed down some stone stairs leading into the chamber and hurriedly began unshackling and releasing the girls.

His hands fumbled with fear as he freed them from the terrible machines, and he turned constantly, checking to see that the villain had not returned to his lair while Ascham was in it.

As he released each girl, he shouted, 'Run! Get out of here!' The terrified girls needed no further urging and they scurried up the steps and out the door, despite their lack of clothing.

Ascham came to the two racks. He shook his head sadly and moved to the last girl, the one wearing the eyeless iron helmet.

His fingers quivering, Ascham unlatched the dreadful mask and removed it, revealing a beautiful young woman with dark eyes, olive skin and long brown hair.

The king's lost girl.

'Isabella?' he asked.

'*Si* . . . yes,' she said through teary eyes.

'Come on.'

He pulled her to her feet and, leading her by the hand, clambered up the stone steps and raced outside.

He emerged to find snow still falling and the sky darkening. He stepped onto the bridge. They had to get out of the forest before nightfall—

'I love to know the inner workings of things,' a voice said through the gloom, stopping him dead.

Ascham looked up and saw a lone figure standing at the far end of the bridge spanning the frozen pond. The women he had freed had not yet crossed the bridge for the figure was blocking it, their only avenue of escape.

Ascham froze, for he had heard those very same words earlier that day from those very same lips.

It was the Earl of Cumberland's bastard son, the student named Timothy Higginbotham.

'I see that you have found my private surgery, Mr Ascham,' Higginbotham said evenly.

'It is the lair of one with a warped mind,' Ascham said.

'I like to think of it as an inquiring mind,' the lad said. 'I wish to become the finest surgeon in England. Think of this as extra study on my part.'

Ascham sized up the lad as he spoke. He was tall and strong but certainly no match for a warrior like Sir Roderick. Ascham wondered how he had got the better of Roderick.

'What sort of monster uses other human beings for his experiments?' Ascham said, his eyes roving as he spoke. He saw that the lad had no discernible weapon on him.

'My father introduced me to women like this when I was young,' Higginbotham said. 'He said they would make a man out of me, but they laughed at me. They do not laugh anymore. They beg. And I quite like that. Well, I suppose you have got me, Mr Ascham. You have outwitted me. Come and escort me to the authorities.'

Ascham walked past the horrified and freezing young ladies, stepping further out onto the low wooden bridge, only twenty feet from Higginbotham.

Higginbotham watched as Ascham strode out into the centre of the bridge, and then suddenly the boy lunged to his left and threw a hidden lever.

The middle section of the bridge dropped away, as if on a hinge, plunging into the ice-covered pond.

The lad looked up, grinning, no doubt keen to see Ascham drop into the freezing waters—

—only there was Ascham, standing on the left-side beam of the bridge, having leapt onto it at the last instant, safe from the open trap-door beside him.

Higginbotham's grin faded.

'Sir Roderick drowned before he froze, boy,' Ascham said. 'There had to be some way you got the better of him, some way you managed to drop him into a body of water from which he could not escape—like a trap-door into an ice-covered pond.'

Higginbotham turned and ran.

Ascham gave chase, edging across the rest of the bridge via the side beam before dashing down the trail as the snow fell harder and the day grew darker.

He was approaching a bend at speed when suddenly the lad's fist came rushing at him from behind a tree. The blow hit home and Ascham's feet flew out from under him and he hit the ground with a great ungainly thump.

Dazed and in pain, he looked up to see the Earl's son standing over him. The lad had picked up a sizeable rock and held it in his hand like a weapon.

'I cannot allow you to leave this place alive,' Higginbotham said. 'Rest assured, though, that you will be found . . . a long way from here.'

Ascham scrambled on his rear-end along the dirt trail, away at the lad's boots as they advanced. He rolled away, desperate, before suddenly he stopped and looked back up at his assailant and said, 'Only one of us will be leaving this place, lad. And it will be me.'

With those words, Ascham lashed out with his right hand and broke the trip-rope crossing the path just behind him.

The swingblade came rushing down and just as the lad comprehended what Ascham had done—that he had got the better of him—the scythe-blade cut cleanly through his neck and the villain fell to the ground, headless, a bucket's worth of blood splashing onto the yellow-flecked dirt all around him.

Still lying on the path, Ascham could only stare in wonder, breathless wonder, at what he had just done.

'Goodness me . . .' he gasped. 'Goodness gracious me.'

his favourite girl was....

were not the days...

exterminated, was...

killed this late in...

College, it has...

7

Once he had recovered from the shock of his encounter with the deranged Higginbotham, Ascham escorted the young women he had rescued to the safety of a local convent.

There, with the aid of the resident nuns, he attended to the poor women, ensuring they were clothed and fed. He only left when the last one was asleep, in safety, warmth and comfort.

While he did this, he sent word to the king that the Italian girl, Isabella, had been found, along with a summary of the acts of the Earl of Cumberland's bastard son, who had taken to kidnapping, torturing and performing surgery on prostitutes from Cambridge and its surrounding towns.

He also mentioned the manners of Sir Roderick's and Napier senior's deaths, and confirmed that Higginbotham had unfortunately been killed in the course of the investigation.

After Ascham was satisfied that the girls were in safe hands, he made his way to King's College to face King

Henry, certain that His Majesty, while pleased to know his favourite girl was safe, would want a comprehensive report of the day's events—the death of an Earl's son, even a bastard, was not a matter that was taken lightly.

It was thus late in the evening when Ascham arrived at King's College, exhausted and cold, to be informed that King Henry had only an hour previously hurried back to London to deal with some pressing matter of state.

And so Ascham found himself standing at the doors to King's College on a snowy winter's night, having confronted a monster on behalf of a king who was no longer there to hear his report. He wondered if the king even remembered the commission he had given Ascham that morning.

Ascham sighed and trudged back to his rooms.

The next morning, Princess Elizabeth, fresh from her lesson with Giles, challenged Ascham to a game of chess.

As Bess set up the pieces, she asked, 'Whatever did you get up to yesterday? You were gone all afternoon and evening.'

'I shall tell you about it some day,' Ascham said with a sad smile, 'but now is not the time. Come, let us play. It's your move.'